A DYLAN M

MONSTER
IN THE
MOUNTAINS

SHANE PEACOCK

NIMBUS
PUBLISHING

Nimbus Publishing Limited
3660 Strawberry Hill Street, Halifax, NS, B3K 5A9
(902) 455-4286 nimbus.ca

Printed and bound in Canada

NB1390

MIX
Paper from
responsible sources
FSC® C013916

Cover design: Cyanotype Books
Interior design: Jenn Embree

Library and Archives Canada Cataloguing in Publication
    Title: Monster in the mountains / Shane Peacock.
    Names: Peacock, Shane, author.
    Description: "A Dylan Maples adventure". | Originally published: Toronto : Puffin Canada, 2003.
    Identifiers: Canadiana (print) 20189068299 | Canadiana (ebook) 20189068302 | ISBN 9781771087155 (softcover) | ISBN 9781771087162 (HTML)
    Classification: LCC PS8581.E234 M68 2019 | DDC jC813/.6—dc23

Nimbus Publishing acknowledges the financial support for its publishing activities from the Government of Canada, the Canada Council for the Arts, and from the Province of Nova Scotia. We are pleased to work in partnership with the Province of Nova Scotia to develop and promote our creative industries for the benefit of all Nova Scotians.

For my friends, the Prince of the Air and the Great Farini:
Jay Cochrane and William Hunt.
Forever young.

"There's no use trying," [Alice] said, "one can't believe impossible things."

"I daresay you haven't had much practice," said the Queen. "When I was your age, I always did it for half an hour a day. Why, sometimes I've believed as many as six impossible things before breakfast."

Lewis Carroll, *Through the Looking-Glass*

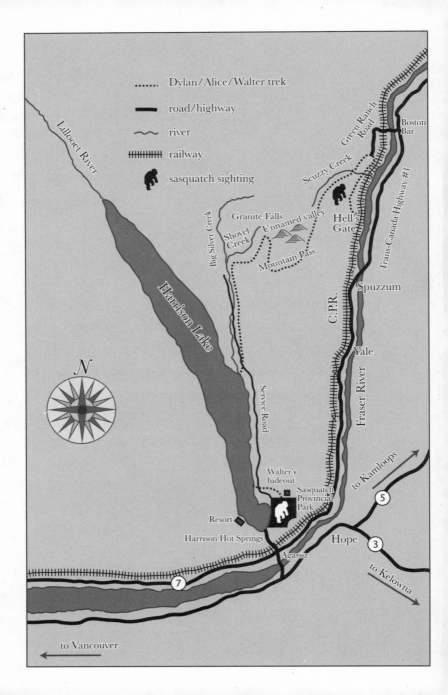

TABLE OF CONTENTS

1

INTO THE UPPER WORLD

Walter Middy tossed and turned. His eyes flickered beneath his closed lids, racing back and forth inside his sockets. His bed was wet with sweat in the warm BC night. It ran along his brow and trickled down his cheeks. His dream had come again. The monster was in the woods. He saw it through the dark shadows, the shades of green, staring at him. Walter Middy came suddenly awake. Now his eyes were as wide as moons. He sat on the edge of his bed, his heart thumping.

KICKING BACK. THAT'S WHAT I was trying to do. I'd just been through this harrowing experience of getting my butt lost in Dinosaur Provincial Park in southern Alberta, and then being chased by this weirdo called "the Reptile." Now he was on his way back to jail, and my parents, who had rushed out west from our home in Toronto like a couple of mother wolves, were back in charge of me. Usually at fourteen you don't like to think of Ma and Pa as running your life. But I'd had enough adventure to last me a long, long time. So I was chillin'...working on it, anyway.

I had draped myself across the back seat of our rented Jeep, the seat belt kind of on. The tunes were exploding from a playlist I'd put on Mom's phone and rocketing into my head—whenever I can get them bouncing off my eardrums like that, doing them serious damage, man, that's the best. The sky was clear blue and distant, like it always seems in Alberta, and I was watching the world go by. Every now and then I'd think about the Reptile, seven feet tall with a shaved head, tracking down me and my buddies in that desert-like park, holding us captive until we escaped. It seemed like a nightmare to me, not something that really happened. It was still freaking me out. But I just couldn't admit that to Mom and Dad. After a while, I started thinking about it too much. The Reptile's face was in my head.

I couldn't concentrate on the tunes any more, so I took off the earphones and snuggled down into the seat, curled up, kind of hugging myself. That blue sky was passing over. I was tired out, so wasted....

I THOUGHT I HEARD A SOUND in the distance, like the squawk of a goose or something. It took a while before I realized what it was.

It was Mom. She was turning to look back at me, with this sweet smile on her face. It's the one she uses when she's trying to look "pleasant," as she says. Normally, she'd be pretty upset by the fact that I'd been spending my time lying on the back seat listening to music while we were driving through a place I'd never seen before. Mom and Dad expect me to at least glance out the window when we're travelling. But here she was with that great big smile. Her head seemed like it had swivelled around so it was on backwards. She was looking right at me.

I sat up. I felt dizzy at first, but then everything in the Jeep cleared up. In fact, it got very clear.

"We're nearing the mountains, sweetie. Care to take a look?"

Why we're heading west towards the Rocky Mountains of British Columbia, instead of east in a plane from Calgary to home, is another story. Mom and Dad are always worried about something they call my "well-being." And after what I'd been through in Alberta, they were absolutely paranoid about it. They thought I needed some time off. And they were right. A trip to BC, they told me, is like a trip into another world, where everything and everyone is totally relaxed. It's more beautiful in British Columbia, they said, than I could imagine.

"Its gorgeous," said Mom.

"It's Lotusland, buddy," said Dad. "It's Wonderland."

"Mountains," said Mom.

"Giant trees," said Dad.

"Nature!" they said together.

Yeah, yeah, yeah. As long as I get to catch some rays, play some tunes, maybe put in some swim time, great. I just wanted to relax. I doubted my parental units really understood what that meant. They'd packed a tent and three sleeping bags into the Jeep. They're into that kind of back-to-nature stuff. Most adults from the city are. But it sort of makes me puke.

"So, what do you think?" asked Dad, pointing out the front window towards our destination.

"Nice. Nice mountains, Dad."

"Are you really looking at them?" inquired Mom. She reads me like a book.

So, I took a look. And I must admit, I was kind of blown away. We were nearing a town called Canmore, getting close to the BC border. They were mountains all right, a wall of them approaching from the distance. I'd seen lots of mountains on TV and in movies, but man, these were *real* mountains. They loomed like rocky monsters in the sky. And as we moved towards them they kept getting bigger and bigger. It was June, but I could actually see snow way, way up on their distant peaks.

I'd been reading a bit about BC, using this guidebook Mom and Dad had purposely left on the back seat that morning. They think it's important to study every place you go to. I started leafing through it, reading bits here and there. It actually had some neat stuff in it. BC has rainforests and beautiful lakes...and lots of legends about weird creatures that live there. In fact, the British Columbia Cryptozoology Club claims that its province has more unclassified animals than any place in the world. Just what I need...monsters. But I read on, to a page headlined "Demons of the Deep." It described BC's famous sea serpents—like the gigantic Cadborosaurus, which haunts the Pacific coastline, and the awesome Ogopogo, the huge prehistoric snake that lives in Okanagan Lake. Some claim its black-and-green torso twists up above the blue waters to this day, its horse-like head surfacing in plain sight.

I turned the page.

BC's greatest monster, the one and only sasquatch, terror of the forests, was staring back at me. The first sentence said there was evidence it really existed.

I closed the book. My pulse was quickening.

I'd been kind of freaked out by stories like this long before I went to Alberta: by ghosts and weird, lurking creatures. I used to hate the dark when I was a little kid and I guess I hadn't entirely grown out of it. In the old days, I was the worst guy for thinking there were monsters in my closet or under my bed. Now I dream up other things. I'm cursed with a wild imagination. My nightmare in Alberta hadn't helped matters.

"We'll be in Banff in twenty minutes," remarked Dad, who had the map pinned between his legs. He's a lawyer: John A. Maples, always full of information and opinions. Mom's a private-school teacher: Laura S., a bit of a hugger and kisser. As he talked, she kept glancing back at me.

"Banff has a population of 8,666 granola-loving souls," Dad explained, sounding, as usual, like he was reading from a tourist pamphlet. "It is home to one of the country's most spectacular CP Hotels, opened in 1888, just after Sir John A. Macdonald put his legendary railway through the mountains. It looks like a huge Canadian castle in the wilderness."

I didn't care about any castle in the wilderness just then…unless it had a hot tub.

"Would you like to camp out tonight, honey?"

Mom wouldn't usually give me a choice like that. It showed how careful she and Dad were being about my feelings. I had even heard them use the word "fragile" about me. In a way, that sounded great. The more fragile I could be, the more I could make things break in my direction.

"Uh, maybe not tonight, Mom. Could we stay in the hotel?"

"That," exclaimed Dad, "is a fine idea, champ!"

He actually calls me champ. Sill.

Funny thing about this place in the wilderness: you get to it on a four-lane highway. But the coolest thing about it was entering it through the mountains. It was the weirdest feeling. It was like we fell into a hole or something that had no bottom: except we went skyward, pulled up the road into a fantasy world. Into Wonderland, I suppose.

Things started to get very weird from that moment on.

The elk wandering around on the streets of Banff should have told me something. By that I don't mean that the elk should have been talking to me, though by the time my trip to BC was over that would have made perfect sense. I just mean that elk casually strolling down the main drag of the place didn't even raise an eyebrow from the locals. The Americans, and there was a pile of them in Banff, kind of stared at them with their mouths wide open. Mom and Dad were all giddy about the elk in a different way and kept telling me that this was how life should be, that nature should "co-exist" with human beings. But I bet Dad would have called the police if one of those things had wandered into our backyard in Toronto, especially if it pooped on Mom's "organic" garden. Here, they were "magnificent creatures."

Banff is a sort of paradise for people with money. There's lots of stuff to buy: clothes, skiing gear, fancy food. And chocolate stores everywhere. Some looked like they were made out of candy. The Tweedledum and Tweedledee Emporium was the best. It was designed like a rainforest inside, with spooky animal sounds and thunder bursts and candies hanging from the trees; candies they claimed were both "healthy and sweet." The old bookstores with the wooden floors were neat too, with stuffed Harry Potters and Gandalfs peering out windows like they were alive. One store had a Humpty Dumpty falling off the front door.

Mom and Dad decided to take me to a museum. For most kids that would be a big drag, but I actually don't hate museums, not too much anyway. History kind of gets my juices flowing. I know that's strange. But I just can't get over how freaky the past seems. And this place had one thing that *really* got to me.

I was walking along looking at the five millionth exhibit about the Canadian Pacific Railway being built through the mountains, getting a bit bored, when I suddenly saw a monster, *the* monster. I spotted it clean across a room and turned and walked slowly towards it. Behind the glass I could see some plastic trees, some fake dirt, and then this amazing face staring over at me. I went right up to the exhibit and put my nose so close to the glass that my breath made a circle of fog on it. The creature looked like a huge ape, but there was something human about it, especially in its eyes, THE SASQUATCH read the sign. "The Salish people, indigenous to this beautiful land, called it Sesquac, a wild beast that lives in the forests and is better off left alone. In the United States it is known as Bigfoot. It is just one of the many legendary creatures that live in British Columbia." I looked deeply into its wild face. A wave of fear came over me. How could I be so frightened of a model in a museum?

Then, out of nowhere, I heard a little girl's voice.

"My father told me that when he was young, all the children who grew up in British Columbia were told stories about the sasquatch, and believed in it," she said. Her voice sounded like one you'd hear in a dream. She was so close that she seemed to be standing right beside me, but when I turned to look at her, there was no one there. Then I realized Dad was saying something.

"Dylan?...Dylan? Wake-ee, wake-ee. Never seen a monster before?"

"Uh, yeah."

"Don't tease him," whispered Mom to Dad. She didn't look too pleased. But Dad walked up and clapped his arm around me. He had his own way of trying to make me feel better: his man-to-man solution.

"You'd think they could do a better job than that," he snickered. "If that thing had come out of my closet, or out from under the bed when I was a kid, I think I would have died laughing."

"Yeah, me too."

"I'd put the sasquatch on par with Santa Claus," he smirked. "Man, that looks fake." He turned and walked away. But I just stood there. Mom gave my arm a squeeze and then rapped him on the elbow when she caught up to him.

A few minutes later I was still standing near the exhibit. "Uh, Dylan?" Mom called from across the room. "Let's get to the hotel." She looked a little worried.

I moved away, glancing back at the sasquatch. When I tried to find Mom, she was gone. I guess she and Dad were doing that thing they often do: giving me "some space." I walked like a bit of a zombie, feeling spooked even though I knew Dad was right about how fake the exhibit looked. I wanted to give my head a shake and knock out my fear.

Soon I heard Mom's and Dad's voices near the exit. As I moved towards them I passed a mirror labelled THE LOOKING GLASS. On its frame was a button with a slot. "You've Seen the Past, Now Look into Your Future," it said. Twenty-five cents. I pulled out a quarter, dropped it into the slot, and pushed the button. A card immediately came out.

Beware of the monsters in your mind. They are here in Wonderland.

Mom and Dad walked behind me back down the main street. The mountains loomed over the town. The hotel was in front of us, a castle on the horizon. Mom lowered her voice, but I caught bits of what she was saying. Something about me still being in shock from last week.

I clutched the fortune card in my hand. It was wet with my sweat. Something didn't make sense. I didn't believe anyone could predict the future, but I was starting to get the awful feeling that something bizarre was going to happen to me on this trip. I felt like I was falling into something bad…and I couldn't do anything about it.

2

LAND OF DREAMS

The next day we were up early and drove to a place called Lake Louise, about a spitball shot from the BC border. As we approached it, going through the Bow Valley on the Trans-Canada Highway, Mom and Dad were getting even more excited. We were about to really get back to nature.

Ever since a few kilometres east of Banff, we had been in a national park. There's a whole series of them out there, full of wild animals, mountains, trees, lakes… and all sorts of old people like my parents who want to walk around in the trees, hugging them, and getting teary-eyed looking at the water. Dad said nine million people came there every year.

The hotel where we stayed, the giant Château Lake Louise, up a really steep road into nowhereland, was actually pretty neat. The lake was right in front of it. It had this colour to it, sort of blue but not blue like any lake I'd ever seen—it kind of glowed. There were tourists from all over the world there, staring and taking millions of pictures, and tons of fake Mounties and beavers, of course.

Mom and Dad insisted we do some hiking. We climbed a path that led into the mountains, where we found some alpine lakes. One was as smooth as glass and called Mirror Lake. Legend has it that wild goats used to come there to look at their reflections and comb their beards. That kind of fit the place.

We hit the road early the following morning, and within ten minutes we entered BC. BRITISH COLUMBIA, LAND OF DREAMS, read a big blue sign. We went in through a "pass" in the mountains. These passes are like giant cuts through the rocks that Indigenous people used in the old days and that the Canadian Pacific Railway followed to get to Vancouver. This one had a great name: Kicking Horse Pass. Dad went on and on at this point about how they built the CPR. He said that all sorts of scandals and heroes came out of it, that they had to blast their way through the mountains, that people died scouting it out and building it, that guys with bizarre names like Cornelius Van Horne and Sir Sandford Fleming and "Hell's Bells" Rogers helped do it—all to bind Canada together from coast to coast.

I didn't listen to all of what he said, but looking out the window and catching sight of the railway tracks winding along through the mountains really made my imagination run wild. It must have been quite the trip building that thing.

"Selkirk Mountain Range, Rogers Pass, population zero," barked Dad from the pilot seat.

I caught sight of another sign going by. AVALANCHE AREA, DO NOT STOP, it warned.

"What does that mean?" I asked shakily. "Are we going to get nailed by an avalanche?"

"No, not in the summer," said Mom.

"It's the mudslides you've got to worry about this time of the year," added Dad absent-mindedly, glancing over at his map. "A man was killed just up the road last week. Buried alive. Never found his body."

"That was...uh," responded Mom, glancing back at me and almost snarling at Dad, "*very* unusual."

It was incredible. Here we were on a narrow two-lane highway in the mountains, going through these long tunnels that protected us from falling boulders and mud and snow, and every building we passed looked like a tunnel itself, covered up for protection. I gazed out the window and wondered what else lurked in these wilds.

"You know, dear, there are eagles around here, and mule deer and mountain goats," said Mom on cue, sounding cheery.

"Are there any grizzlies?" I asked, "or black bears?"

"Very few," replied Mom quickly.

"And the sasquatch, of course," laughed Dad, hoping I'd laugh with him. But I kept staring out the window, trying to think good thoughts.

Just past Revelstoke and the cavernous Three Valley Gap, we spotted some bighorn sheep standing like high-wire walkers on the sides of the rocks. Waterfalls poured down from the heights in places, where the summits were three thousand metres high. Gigantic rock faces peered at me. A train came steaming along near us and disappeared into a tunnel like a snake crawling into the mountains. We were going around breakneck corners—where I could just see us flipping over and flying off the road into the canyons—and driving down long, steep hills where Dad had to brake to keep from speeding out of control. It would be perfect for a James Bond movie; I started thinking about bad guys racing after us.

Suddenly the Reptile's face flashed through my brain. I felt for that fortune card in my pocket. *Beware of the monsters in your mind. They are here in Wonderland.* I gazed into the mountain wilderness, feeling freaked out again.

Monsters.

I noticed that Mom was watching me again. Soon she was bringing up any happy thing she could think of, talking about the rest of the trip to Vancouver (we'd fly home from there), saying it would be fabulous.

"We have a surprise for you, too. It's something we're going to do before we get to the coast." The expression on her face made me think I'd like it.

"We'll tell you soon."

A few hours later we started going downward and entered a sort of paradise in the mountains. It was like something out of a dream. The Okanagan Valley just suddenly appeared, looking like California on a hot day: fruit trees were everywhere and beautiful lakes; everyone had a tan, girls were wearing bikinis and guys, shorts. We zoomed south into the city of Kelowna and then over Okanagan Lake on a floating bridge, above the depths where Ogopogo is supposed to live. We stayed overnight in Peachland, on the west side of the lake. In the morning I stood on the beach next to the blue water and stared out across the flat surface. It glinted here and there, sparkling in the sun. Dad had picked up a local pamphlet and was reading it as he walked up to me. He pointed to "Rattlesnake Island" in the distance.

"That's where their sea monster lives." He chuckled.

I gazed out. Were they just glints of light playing off the water? Or was something moving out there, rolling through the waves?

We drove south along the Okanagan. Then we turned west and the land changed. But I barely noticed. My nose was buried in the guidebook again. One of the photos in the monsters chapter was mesmerizing me. Looking through the rear-view mirror, Dad noticed. He tipped it down so he could see what I was stuck on.

Sasquatch.

"Remember what I told you when you were, oh, about two years old, son? *There are no real monsters.* Here's a news flash for you: dragons never walked the face of the earth."

"Why don't you just relax, Dylan," said Mom, giving Dad a stare, "and look at the scenery while I tell you about our surprise." I had the feeling that she'd wanted to leave this until later, but was getting desperate to make me feel better.

I glanced outdoors. It was a beautiful green area of rolling hills that flattened out in places, amazing since we were still in the mountains. We might as well have been travelling through locations for cowboy movies, filled with valleys where cattle grazed. Everything was so green it looked like a painting. I couldn't stop feeling like the world going past my window wasn't real.

Mom smiled at Dad. "We are going to stay at a resort," she said. "And we'll be there by late this afternoon."

I set the book down. "A resort?" That sounded good.

"It's in a place called Harrison Hot Springs, population—"

"We don't need to know the population, John, just this once."

"Right," said Dad, reacting a bit like a kid who'd had his hand slapped.

"It's a beautiful spot with hot springs and a huge hotel and a beach and little restaurants and live bands and sand sculpture contests, sitting in front of a gorgeous lake, surrounded by mountains."

"And Sasquatch Provincial Park!" cracked Dad.

"What?"

"A beach and bands and…."

"No, no. The park. What's it called?"

Dad turned around and gave me an evil glare. "Sssssssasssssssquatch Provincial Park!"

"Why do they call it that?"

"Why do you think?" inquired Dad in a horror-movie voice, swivelling his head right around like Mom had earlier. He was trying awfully hard to make the whole thing sound childish.

"Please watch the road, Johnny. Sometimes I think Dylan's about twice your age."

She reached back and patted me on the knee.

"Oh, there're stupid stories about the sasquatch being around there," she said.

"Seen more often near Harrison Lake and the park than any other place in the world."

"Really?" I asked.

"Dylan," said Dad in his regular voice, "you can't be seriously interested in such nonsense. The sasquatch monster? What's next, the abominable snowman?"

"That's Yeti. He's from the Himalaya Mountains, Dad, not Canada."

"He's from Mars. Just like the sasquatch...and Ogopogo."

I opened the guidebook and turned back to the section I'd been glued to. There was that picture again: a reproduction of a single frame of a film. It showed a sasquatch walking away, glaring back over its shoulder at whoever was holding the camera. It was supposed to be real, taken somewhere near the west coast by two guys named Roger Patterson and Bob Gimlin with a sixteen-millimetre movie camera in 1967. I just couldn't get over it. Could this thing really exist?

It took us another few hours to get to Harrison Hot Springs. We passed through an area that used to be the centre of a gold and silver rush, then entered Manning Provincial Park and began a long drop out of the mountains towards the Fraser River and its canyon. I couldn't believe how high up we had been. It seemed to take us forever to get down. We saw warning signs for truck drivers along the road. Rough ramps were cut out of the trees on the sides of the highway so that out-of-control transports could veer off and go up into the woods to stop.

I looked out into the dense forest. At times, things seemed to be moving in the trees.

Sasquatch.

"Before we get to Harrison, we need to tell you something," said Mom, looking over at Dad.

She sounded pretty serious.

"What?"

"Well, you have an uncle in Harrison Hot Springs.

A great-uncle—named Walter Middy. He's Grandma Secord's brother. She was a Middy before she married."

"Yeah. So?"

Mom and Dad exchanged glances again.

"Well, we just thought we'd tell you. We might drop by his place and say hello. That's it. It would just be a short meeting. You don't even have to come."

They don't want me to meet an uncle I've never even seen before? That was strange. They're usually pretty big on family. Was this guy scary or something?

"He's kind of weird," said Dad.

"Weirder than you guys?"

There was a pause. Then they laughed. They sounded relieved to hear me tell a joke. At least they thought it was a joke. No one was much weirder than the parental units.

They were making me curious about my uncle. But really, I'd had enough of weird people. It would be fine with me if the rest of this trip and the rest of my life were totally boring.

I was actually starting to feel a little better about things by then. Our surroundings weren't nearly as wild. We had finally reached the Fraser River, and a good old four-lane highway was stretching out in front of us, running towards Vancouver. You could feel the population picking up, the spookier land disappearing behind us. We drove into a town called Hope and then crossed over the river to the north side. Five minutes later we passed a sign that read SASQUATCH PROVINCIAL PARK. There it was, in plain English. I actually rubbed my eyes and looked at it twice. It *really* existed.

Once we turned off the main road and headed away from the river, I could almost feel Harrison Hot Springs approaching. It just felt different. It seemed hot, almost tropical, like we were going into a Canadian jungle. And the sasquatch was suddenly everywhere. There was Bigfoot Campground, Sasquatch Springs RV Resort, hairy monster faces staring out from signs, and big wood carvings of giant beasts standing by the roadside. Everybody was making a buck from the legend.

Soon we slowed down and approached the town, then turned at the beach. The blue lake looked like a huge long bathtub, with a hilly island in the middle and mountains rising on all sides. Sailboats dotted the surface and sunbathers were everywhere. A little on the stunning side, I had to admit. The resort hotel was off to our left, up the beach. It was made up of a couple of tall new buildings on either side of an old one. It was all brick and green gables. We pulled up in front of the main doors and a bellhop came running out to help us. Service. Things were looking up.

But as I leapt out, I glanced back down the beach, past a big round swimming pool that looked like a massive bowl embedded in the sand, and had the strange feeling that someone was watching me. Another wave of fear swept through me as I searched the distant crowd. But in seconds it all passed.

3

THE MAGNIFICENT MIDDY

A solid afternoon of swimming at that big flying saucer in the beach, while music roared out of various speakers up and down the boardwalk, made me forget my worries for a while. People were parasailing around in the sky, there were Sea-Doos rocking the waves and all sorts of cool stuff. Then, at night, we caught some lounging time in the hot springs pools in this garden area behind the resort. It was unbelievable, like being in a gigantic hot tub. They keep them open late into the night. The parental units and I even went for a dip—well, more like a soak—not long before the stroke of midnight. Man, that was really kicking back.

These springs are the reason the whole place exists. The Salish First Nations knew there was natural hot water rising up from the ground long before the white man even came here. They believed it had healing powers. Adventurers started using Harrison Lake as a way to get up north to the Cariboo Gold Rush in the 1850s, then someone jumped into a pond on the way home and discovered how incredibly warm it was, hot really. In fact, the hotel has to cool the water or it would cook human beings. The year after the CPR went through, along the Fraser, they built the first resort at St. Alice Springs, as they called Harrison back then. People came to cure their illnesses. To them, it was a magical place.

Dad, of course, was telling me all this stuff. Magical place? I suppose. Good to hang out in, that's all I knew. But after a day of lying around, I was getting a bit bored. It was proof of how much better I was feeling. Maybe the hot springs were curing me?

Meanwhile, Mom and Dad hadn't said anything else about weird Walter Middy. But I found myself wondering about him. How terrible could my own uncle be? Why hadn't they taken me over to meet him yet? It seemed like they were putting it off. So, finally, I brought up the subject.

"Well…" said Mom. She looked at me for a long time. "What do you think, John?"

That's never a good sign. When they ask each other a question in front of me it means that the one doing the asking doesn't want to deal with the situation. Dad gave her one of his famous firm answers.

"Uh, yeah, okay, I guess," he responded, his head buried in a magazine about mountain climbing.

Mom went into the other room in our suite and came back out a few minutes later.

"We're meeting him at the Muddy Waters Café."

"Neutral ground?" smirked Dad.

"Neutral ground. Six o'clock," replied Mom, not smiling.

A COUPLE HOURS LATER we turned into a café partway down the beach. People were eating their meals out in the sun. But Mom gave a very fake, cheery wave at a table tucked away in a corner. I couldn't make out the form at first, positioned as it was in the shadows. All I saw was a pair of binoculars on a table.

"It isn't that your uncle Walter is a bad person; don't get me wrong," Mom whispered to me as we approached. "He would never hurt you, far from it. It's just that ever since he was a kid he's been involving himself and everyone around him in trouble. So, he wouldn't be the best guy for you to, uh, hang out with. We have no idea what he might get you into. It's like he's never grown up."

Uncle Walter Middy was sitting there in the shadows all right. But he wasn't what I expected. He kind of had his head down and almost seemed shy. When he saw us, he looked quickly at Mom and Dad and then for an instant stared right at me. He had riveting eyes: almost purple. He stood up and nearly knocked a chair over. I could hear him apologize under his breath. This was my scary uncle?

"Laura, dear," he said quietly to Mom, extending a hand that seemed to be shaking a little. "John, it's a pleasure to see you again," he told Dad.

I caught my parents glancing at each other with a slight look of surprise.

Walter Middy turned to me.

"This must be the King of Hearts," he said kindly and shook my hand. It was a gentle squeeze.

"D-Dylan," I stuttered. "Dylan Maples."

I thought he'd be dressed in loud clothing and have a booming voice, but he was quiet in nearly every way: His clothes were as ordinary as they get. He was wearing plain corduroy pants and a short-sleeved golf shirt, both grey. He looked to be about sixty years old, but slim and muscular. His hair was jet black, only slightly streaked with grey. It hung down almost to his shoulders. A long moustache twirled out to two sharp points above a thick goatee. He was an ordinary guy with the face of a Musketeer, like the dashing D'Artagnon. But his days of adventure seemed long gone.

He pulled out chairs for us and we sat. Mom and Dad positioned me between them. As my butt touched the leather I found myself looking straight over Middy's shoulders towards a girl who was looking back at me; she sat at a table facing a woman she didn't seem to be talking to. The girl was about my age, maybe a little older, her hair as black as a raven's. She started to smile at me. I quickly turned my eyes back to Uncle Walter.

"Welcome to Harrison Hot Springs, Maples young and old," he said with a slight smile.

Then he looked down. He did a lot of that while we talked. Sometimes it was even hard to tell what he was saying.

"So, Walter, how have you been?" asked Dad, with a smile as fake as the Cheshire Cat's.

Walter paused for a second, took a deep breath.

"I'm fine...how are you?"

For a while after that the whole conversation was of almost zero interest to me. All adult stuff about "how's the family?" and politics and the weather. I could tell that Uncle Walter wasn't into it either. Oh, he tried to look interested, but every now and then I caught his eyes darting towards me. Then he'd look away. It was like his mind was somewhere else. He looked guilty about something, and very sad. Finally, he interrupted Dad.

"I have to be honest with you," he blurted out.

"Sorry?"

"I know you didn't want to see me today, and I don't blame you."

"Uncle Walter...we, uh, wanted to see you. Didn't we, John?" asked Mom, her "pleasant" smile pasted on her face.

"Sure," said Dad sheepishly.

"I'm grateful that you made the effort and I'm really happy to have met Dylan." He glanced at me. "But don't worry. You can leave any time you want. And you don't have to see me again. I know now that my life has been full of bad choices. I know I'm a bad example. It's taken me years to realize that. I guess wisdom comes with old age. Things are much quieter now. There's no circus in my life any more. I'm not putting anyone else in danger...I'm glad you've given me this opportunity to apologize."

"There's no need for that," said Mom.

"Oh, yes there is. I wish you all well. And I'm sorry."

Circus? Putting people in danger? What was he talking about?

He stood up to go. For the first time I noticed he was wearing hiking boots—they looked a little muddy.

"Sit down, Walter," said Dad.

After that they spoke differently. It was all really emotional stuff about Mom's family. Soon Walter started telling them about his new life in Harrison Hot Springs, how he spent most of his time just walking along the beach, playing a little golf, taking things easy.

Then Dad tried to lighten things up.

"Seen the sasquatch at all?"

Uncle Walter's face went a bit white. He didn't answer. He glanced at me again. Those purple eyes were saying something.

After a long, awkward pause, Mom came to the rescue.

"Well," she said, "we should be going."

"It was great to have seen you. Goodbye," said my uncle in a near-whisper.

"Oh, jabberwocky, Walter, I'm sure we'll be getting together again," grinned Dad, looking at Mom and me.

"Absolutely," said Mom, patting Walter on the hand. "We'll be here for about a week. We're giving Dylan some time off from school."

Then they got all kissy-kissy as we stood up to go. But I had something else on my mind.

"I need to take a leak."

"Pardon me?" asked Mom, looking at me in horror.

"May I please be excused to use the washroom?"

"Yes you may."

When I returned, my parents were already outside waiting for me. Uncle Walter was still at his table, just kind of staring off towards the beach. I walked over to him.

"Uncle Walter?"

He turned and looked into my eyes.

"How you feeling, White Knight?" he asked suddenly, looking concerned.

He'd caught me off guard.

"Uh...okay."

"Really? You don't look so good."

I could have said the same thing about him.

"I'm all right. Had a rough time last week."

"Well, that was last week, wasn't it? This week is

full of new and better possibilities." He said it as if he didn't quite believe it.

"Sure."

There was a pause as we looked at each other.

"Uh, when Dad asked you about seeing the sasquatch, you didn't say anything."

"No."

"Why?"

"Because I don't like to lie."

AS MOM AND DAD and I headed back up the boardwalk towards the resort in the warm evening air, they were both going on and on about the changes in Uncle Walter, and how wonderful it all was. I could tell they were feeling a little guilty about how they'd described him to me. I figured it was a good time to ask a particular question.

"Can I go visit him?"

Mom paused for only a second.

"Sure," she said.

"Sure," agreed Dad. "We'll go tomorrow"

I didn't like that "we" stuff. I wanted some time alone to talk with Walter. I had some questions for him. I'd been awfully scared about a lot of things the past week, but the fear was beginning to slip away. Was it the magical waters of Harrison Hot Springs? Or was it something else? When I looked into my uncle Walter's eyes, I had the strange feeling I was looking into my own. He was a shell of what he'd been...and so was I. I felt like I was learning a lesson the second I laid eyes on him. Mom said he'd never grown up, but to me it seemed more like he was old before his time. Something had scared him too, scared him so much that he was afraid of life, afraid of being himself...and so was I.

4

THE DRAGON

Uncle Walter lived in a condominium complex well down Esplanade Avenue, a wide street that borders the beach. When Mom and Dad and I arrived at his door the following morning, he greeted us in his slippers and led us into the living room. The view out his big picture window was amazing, looking over the boardwalk, the sand, and blue water. The mountainous forests of Sasquatch Provincial Park rose in the distance.

Mom and Dad were more interested in the indoor decorations. His rooms were straight out of the 1960s, the walls painted all the colours of the rainbow, lots of psychedelic posters of long-gone bands with long hair.

It made the parental units feel right at home, even though that was just before their time. Some old tunes were playing softly, perfect for them. Soon we were all sitting down on Walter's leather couches and the three of them were having a boring talk about songs from long ago. In minutes they'd turned them up. "I Am the Walrus" by The Beatles and "Somebody to Love" by Jefferson Airplane blared out of the CD player. The music filled the rooms and spilled out through the open windows.

I started glancing around. Down a hallway I caught sight of two old photographs, almost hidden from view. One was of a beautiful woman, dressed up in a glittering circus costume. She stared out from the picture with a strange look in her eyes, like she was almost alive, like she was ready for anything. The other photograph showed a man standing on a high wire at an awesome height above a city street. It looked scary, but amazing. He had dark hair, a goatee, and a moustache that twirled out to two sharp points. The photo had some fancy lettering on it. THE MAGNIFICENT MID—was all I could read. *There's no circus in my life any more.* That's what he'd said.

He caught my eyes wandering towards the photos. I looked away. Meanwhile, Mom and Dad were having a whale of a time listening to the music and talking about it. Much better than Walter, who seemed sad no matter what was going on. After a while, Mom smiled at him and then at me.

"Dylan," said Mom, "how would you like to spend a little time with your great-uncle while we grab some fresh fruit at the market downstairs? In fact, why don't you just meet us back at the hotel? In twenty minutes?"

"Sure," I said, more pleased than I sounded.

Moments later, the two of us were sitting on the balcony watching people walk by, not saying anything. I noticed his hiking boots sitting on a tray nearby, muddy again.

"Don't you NEED somebody to LOVE?" shouted the female lead singer's voice back in the living room. It really was a rockin' tune. Not bad. Uncle Walter didn't seem to be paying much attention to it, though I noticed his foot silently tapping to the beat. After a while he pulled the sliding glass door closed, muffling the sound. He looked up into the green mass of Sasquatch Provincial Park on the horizon.

"Do you believe in impossibilities, Dylan?"

"Uh...what?"

He paused. Then he looked at me. For a second, I thought he was going to really tell me something. Reveal something.

"Never mind," he finally said.

I was going to have to coax him.

"What did you do, Uncle Walter, when you were younger?"

"A lot of stupid things. It really isn't of much interest."

"It is to me."

He turned and looked at me again. He almost smiled.

"When I was a young boy about your age, I ran away from home. I did something that usually only happens in books, or at least happened in books when I was a boy. I ran away with a circus. It made my parents very unhappy. But I learned how to do a lot of things. I walked the high wire, did the flying trapeze, even the mighty sway pole."

"What's that?"

"You get in this little perch, like a basket on a lookout, about thirty metres in the air at the top of a pole that seems like it's made out of rubber. Then you start to make it sway. It will sway all the way to the ground and take you with it, holding on for dear life. Then it snaps you back up."

Wow.

"Mom and Dad wanted to take me to Cirque du Soleil once."

"That's not a real circus. That's a Las Vegas show made up to look artsy. There aren't many real ones any more, shows with imagination that take chances. The circus is supposed to exist at the edges of our minds."

He had been getting a little excited, but made an effort to calm himself.

"That's why they're dangerous...that's why there are accidents, and people die." He paused, looking very sad. "I'm glad I've left that all in the past."

"Did something happen that made you stop?"

For a second he cast his eyes down the hallway towards that picture of the beautiful circus woman.

"It was a lot of things." It was obvious he didn't want to say anything else about it.

I looked down towards the beach and saw the girl I'd noticed at the café last night. She was sitting on the sand, wearing a black bikini, looking rather grown up, staring at me. I stepped back from the edge of the balcony.

"I didn't have a proper life. We travelled from town to town, so I never settled down. My family didn't know where I was for years. I got married a few times, left people behind. I was just after thrills. Your mom will tell you about me. I missed her grandmother's funeral...my own mother." He paused. Then he lowered his eyes, as if he was thinking back into the past. "I remember I used to read minds on one show." He almost smiled again. "And I drove nails into my brain by hammering them up my nostrils—they call it 'the human blockhead' act. Really disgusting."

That sounded wild. "How do you do that?"

He looked at me kind of funny and kept talking.

"I once displayed the world's largest rat."

"Really?"

"Size of a Newfoundland dog."

"What?"

Uncle Walter leaned down close to me and whispered. "It's really an animal from South America. A capybara, but don't tell anyone." He actually did smile that time.

"I exhibited a dragon, too," he said.

"A dragon?"

"Impossible, isn't it? But there are huge lizards that live in the East Indies that fit the bill. Even scientists call them dragons: Komodo dragons. They might as well be living dinosaurs and are as frightening as a T. rex, believe me. They weigh more than I do. They eat people, in fact have been known to kill human beings, bury them, and dig them up and eat more. We had to be a little careful with that specimen."

I peeked over the edge of the balcony and looked down. She was still there, glancing upward, searching for where I'd gone.

"I made a whole pack of money and saw some remarkable things. I owned some circuses by the time I got out of it. But I was irresponsible and reckless about others. I know that now."

"Mom and Dad thought you were weird."

"They're smart people, good people. I had a well-deserved reputation in the family, Dylan. I thought I was living by my heart and my wits, and I suppose I was, but there's more to life than that. At some point you have to grow up. The family thought I was a particularly nasty little boy, and they were right." He paused. "Your parents are from the world of the possible, Dylan. So am I, now. I don't live in a dream any more."

He turned and looked out into the wilderness again.

I wanted to get back to stories about high wires and sway poles and the world's largest rat. But he didn't seem to be interested.

"They say there's something out there, you know." He motioned towards the miles of trees that lined the mountains and went off into the distance of the park.

"What?"

"They have a two-million-dollar reward for anyone who can find it. It's been a standing offer of this community for many years. They think the whole thing's a joke: a publicity ploy to draw tourists. It makes them money."

"It?"

"The sasquatch."

I felt goosebumps rise on my skin.

"But it doesn't exist. That's just a story," I sputtered.

"Lots of stories are true," he said quietly and looked into his apartment. His gaze rested on one of his old posters. "I, uh, used to be interested in it. In my business, the business of wonder, it was a very big prize. The biggest. I came here long ago to look for it. I even exhibited something we called a sasquatch, but it was really just a big hairy man. I wouldn't do that now: I wouldn't even cage a bird."

"You really believe in it?"

He looked into the mountains again. His eyes grew large and the colour drained from his face. An image in his mind was electrifying him.

"No," he whispered.

I looked down at the girl on the beach. She was staring back up.

"I don't believe in dragons any more," said Uncle Walter.

The glass door behind us slid open on its own. The music came surging out. It was that same sixties band again, Jefferson Airplane, but doing a different song, the woman's voice soaring and intense. The bass line was thumping. It was a loud and crackling tune called "White Rabbit," about a weird world where things shrank and expanded, animals spoke, and people talked backwards.

I looked down. Walter Middy's foot was tapping to the beat.

5

ALICE

"**H**e's a druggie."

"Sorry?"

"That old guy you were with. Why were you with him?"

"He's my great-uncle."

I hadn't even gotten all the way out the door of Uncle Walter's condo and she was right there, a beach towel wrapped around her and wet. Now I noticed her blue eyes. They were incredibly blue, like the water of Lake Louise. They almost seemed lit from the inside. There was some sort of makeup, in a bunch of colours like a rainbow, painted on her lids. Her black hair was slicked back from swimming. She had a little tattoo of a unicorn on her hip and a ring in her belly button. Her skin sparkled like she'd thrown gold dust on it. There were freckles on her face.

"Is he as interesting as...you?"

Wow. I'd never met a girl like this. Back home in Toronto the girls have a reputation for being kind of bold, compared with the ones you meet in other towns anyway. But this one was something else. Maybe she was an American.

"You don't even know me. I've got to get going."

"Where to?"

"Back to the hotel. Mom and Dad wanted me back an hour ago."

"Mommy and Daddy?" she said mockingly. "Why don't you be a big boy and hang out with me for a while...uh...."

She paused and stared at me.

"What?"

"This is when you tell me your name."

"Oh! It's, uh...it's...Dylan. Dylan Maples."

"Hi there. I'm Alice. Alice Emily Carr."

She stuck out her hand, took mine in hers, and then squeezed it gently. For a minute, I thought she wasn't going to let go. Finally, I pulled away.

"I really do have to get back...and he's not a druggie."

Mom and Dad had talked to me about drugs a lot. I had this sneaking suspicion that they had done some when they were young. But they said I should never even experiment. And I agreed. I had no desire. Drugs were trouble. They turn you into an idiot. I was going to have to ask Uncle Walter about his views on the subject, though, straight out.

"Yeah, you'd better get home. You look a little wiped out to me. Hard week?"

I didn't respond. I just started walking away, towards the hotel.

"If he isn't a druggie," Alice yelled, "then he's a wizard or something! He's weird enough to be one!"

Yeah, I thought, *and you're following us around.*

I SAW THE "WIZARD" again the next day. Mom and Dad and I were strolling down Esplanade Avenue along the beach, heading for a swim, when we caught sight of him coming out of his condominium in the distance.

"Why don't you say hello," suggested Mom as she watched Walter walking with his head down, his shoulders hunched, carrying something under his arm. She and Dad veered off in the direction of the water. I strode quickly towards Walter.

But someone intercepted him before I got there, and started talking to him. It was Alice Carr. She was wearing pants that had about a million coloured stripes on them and a short top that showed off her belly-button ring and tattoo. She'd painted on some makeup again, and those sparkles glowed on her skin. I could see what Walter had tucked under his arm now: a skateboard. Alice was doing most of the talking.

"Hi, Dylan," said Walter quietly.

"He isn't a druggie," said Alice out loud, smiling at him.

"Never touched a drug in my life," he responded. "At least I had sense about that. You didn't need them in my line of work. Get on a high wire on drugs and you're a dead man. Get on clean, on a thin line between two skyscrapers, and it will thrill you out of your mind."

Skyscrapers.

"I had natural highs like you wouldn't believe," he said.

I believed.

"I like weird," whispered Alice into my ear, smiling at Walter, standing uncomfortably close to me, her breath tickling my lobe. Walter moved back a little.

We started to talk, and drew some more circus stories out of him. As Walter quietly spoke, he absent-mindedly dropped his skateboard down and did some tricks. He was amazingly good at it.

At first Alice was really into what he was telling us, but then she seemed to lose interest. She started looking away from us, towards the beach. I figured that if she could be bold with me, I could be the same with her.

"What are you looking at?" I finally blurted out.

"Nothing," she said abruptly and stopped looking away. She tried to smile but seemed kind of guilty about something.

Walter snapped his skateboard up into the air with his feet and caught it with his hands. "*Nothing* is a pretty boring thing to spend your time looking at."

Alice sighed. "It's my parent. Over there." She nodded towards the beach.

"Parent?"

"The one and only Carol Lewis. Voilà." She pointed out a woman lying in a lounge chair about a hundred metres away. She had blonde hair and was wearing a skimpy bikini. A man, blonde too and younger than her, was applying suntan lotion to her back. She was giggling.

"Just parent? As in, one parent? That guy's not your dad?"

"No no, that's not my dad. He's with someone else

somewhere in Vancouver. I have no idea who *that* is, as usual. My mother likes to exchange one typical adult for another." For a second I thought she was going to cry. But then her eyes widened.

"Uh oh!"

Her mother had spotted her. She was rising and coming towards us. She had taken the man's hand and was pulling him along.

"I'm sorry about this. She'll make me introduce you."

"That's okay," I said, wondering why her mother upset her so much.

They were near us in seconds it seemed.

"Alice, dear, you have a friend," said Carol Lewis after she and her own friend jumped with a laugh over the low stone wall that separated the Esplanade from the beach. They smelled of suntan oil and perfume.

"So do you, Carol," said Alice.

I have a few friends who call their parents by their first names. It seems kind of stupid to me, like the parental units are trying to be kids and suck up to them. My mom's my mom, and my dad's my dad. They aren't anything else, for better or worse. I'd rather be real with them. Alice Carr, who must have her dad's last name, said "Carol" as if it were the name of the most boring person on earth.

"Yes I do, dear, I do," smiled Carol, gritting her teeth. You could tell she wasn't Alice's biggest fan at this moment either. "This is Lance Bennett, proprietor of Tweedledum and Tweedledee Candies." She said this as if it was supposed to impress Alice, raising her eyebrows as she spoke. Alice didn't seem to care. But I did. Tweedledum and Tweedledee! That was the amazing chain of BC stores with candies that were healthy and sweet. Maybe we could score some!

"The organic candy emporium," Lance offered, extending a hand to Alice, which she wouldn't take. I stuck out my hand immediately. Lance grabbed it with relief and nearly busted my fingers with his grip.

"Dylan Maples," I said in the deepest voice I could find.

"Lance Bennett, Mr. Maples," he announced. I almost looked around to see if Dad was standing behind me.

He and Carol stood there looking at me for a few seconds with big grins. She was the kind of woman who really stood out on a beach, with her trendy bathing suit and glowing blonde hair. I glanced over at Alice. You couldn't find two hair colours more different—and it wasn't hard to guess who the fake was.

Lance looked rich. He just had that way about him. He was smooth as cream about everything, right from the way he talked and the knee-length swimsuit he had on to his pitch-black shades and blonde hair and moustache. I could see that Alice hated him, right off.

"I've just met your mother here, Alice, and she's been telling me *all* about you."

"How lovely."

"Uh…yes it is, actually. What are you two up to?"

That reminded me. I supposed it was my job to introduce Uncle Walter. "Mind your manners," Mom would say. I wondered why Lance had said "you two."

"Oh, this is my Uncle Wal—"

As I turned I realized he wasn't there. I glanced around. No Walter. Then I looked across the road towards his condo and up and down the street. No Walter.

"He's—he's gone!" said Alice, just as stunned as me.

"Well, maybe he's shy," laughed Lance.

"He's not shy," snapped Alice, "he's amazing. You should hear all the things he's done! He used to be a high-wire walker!"

Amazing? I doubted it was a word that most people would use about my uncle Walter these days. It sounded funny when she said it, but I agreed.

"Well," purred Carol, "Lance here is pretty amazing himself. He's about to open a brand-new Tweedledum and Tweedledee right in Harrison Hot Springs. The biggest store outside of Vancouver, with a café attached and maybe even a spa for rich Americans. 'Health and Pleasure,' right, Lance? And get this, Alice, he'd like *me* to do the PR."

I knew what that meant: public relations—doing advertising and that sort of stuff for a company.

"That's nice, Carol, but Dylan's uncle is a bit beyond candy stores in terms of amazing."

"Yes, dear, I know, you told us. He's an old circus star."

"He's a lot more than that," she shot back. Alice seemed desperate to come up with something else. She turned to me. "Isn't he, Dylan?"

"Sure, uh…he knows things about the sasquatch." It was all I could think of.

"The what?" asked Carol blankly.

"Really?" inquired Lance abruptly, looking genuinely interested. "That's quite a feature in these parts, isn't it, that tall tale?"

"He says it's real." Alice countered.

I wished she wouldn't have said that. First of all, Uncle Walter had never said it himself. And secondly, he was strange enough without it being broadcast to a PR person and her rich boyfriend.

"Well, good for him." Carol smiled. "What's a sasquatch?"

"Oh, Carol, you bozo."

I couldn't believe Alice had actually said that to her mother. If I'd done it I'd have been grounded for seventy-five years, give or take a decade. It kind of made me cringe.

"On that note," snapped Carol, "Lance and I will vamoose. I will see you, young lady, at the hotel restaurant at six."

"Maybe," said Alice under her breath as her mother clutched Lance's hand and steered them away. But Lance broke loose for a second and hurried back to us.

"Been reading about the monster thing in the flyers they give out around here. Uh, sounds fascinating, really does." Then he rushed off to join Carol, waving back at us a few times.

The way he'd said that was a bit strange. It was like a mixture of someone lying and telling you the absolute truth.

"I *didn't* say that about the sasquatch," said a stern voice.

It was Uncle Walter. Alice and I just about jumped out of our sandals. He was standing right beside us.

"But...but you believe in it, don't you?" Alice stammered.

"Best to leave that legend alone. I'll let the experts decide. And there are lots of them around here."

He didn't seem to be too pleased that Alice was making things up about him, and in another few minutes he was gone. As he moved away, I noticed that he'd changed into his hiking boots. There were pine needles under the laces.

Alice and I walked along the boardwalk. We didn't say anything for a while. We were both thinking.

"What do you figure he meant by there being lots of experts around here?" she finally asked.

"I guess there must be people in Harrison Hot Springs who know a lot about the sasquatch. That makes sense, doesn't it?"

"Let's find one!"

"One what? A sasquatch?" I felt a little twinge of fear.

"No, goof, an expert."

"Why?"

"Did someone hit you on the head or something? We're in a place that holds the answer to the world's greatest monster mystery, and there are people here who know all about it and you want to know why we'd talk to them? Let's check them out. It could be amazing!"

"I'm not really that interested in the sasquatch."

"Yeah right, and I'm the Queen of England."

How could a guy who was scared of everything just days ago, who had spent his whole life dreaming bad dreams about monsters, be interested in the sasquatch? But Alice was right. I *was*. Something was telling me that it was time, right here in Harrison Hot Springs, to face my fears or spend my whole life being afraid. I didn't want to end up like Uncle Walter, turned into a shell of myself. And I knew, deep down, that the sasquatch was one of the coolest things on earth. I'd known it as a kid, and knew it again the second I'd seen its face in that guidebook.

Ten minutes later we were at the Harrison Lake Library. There, sitting on a shelf right at the entrance, was a whole row of books about the sasquatch, all with pictures of horrific-looking monster-apes on their covers. We began flipping to the back of each one, examining the information about the writers. Finally, we found what we were looking for. "The author," the cover read, "lives in Harrison Hot Springs, British Columbia." Soon we discovered three other books by the same guy. We dashed over to the local phone book.

Within a half hour we were walking up to the front door of an ordinary-looking house belonging to one Cosmos Greene.

6

THE SASQUATCH MAN

It wasn't so ordinary inside. And neither was Greene, the sasquatch man. He answered the door and we looked way up. That's because he was about half a foot taller than even Uncle Walter, who's no slouch in the height department. He had this deep voice that seemed to rise out of his chest, and was very hairy. Hair was coming out of his ears, his nose, busting out from under his shirt both back and front, and growing out of the top of his head like a jungle, despite the fact that he was an older guy and grey. He had quite a schnozzola on him too, a big bulbous nose that looked like it should have belonged to a bloodhound, and ears like an elephant's.

He was a little scary at first. We kind of stuttered out why we were there and it seemed like he was scowling at us. But then, for some reason, I brought up Uncle Walter's name. Cosmos Greene grinned, opened the door wide, and invited us in.

Indoors, he gave us a warm smile and shook our hands. Mine just disappeared into his when we gripped. I couldn't believe the size of the mitts on the guy. Then, when he ushered us into his living room, he took these long loping strides. I bet he got to his spot on his big chair in about three steps, and it was on the other side of the room.

There were pictures of the sasquatch all over the place: drawings, photographs, all sorts of things. But the biggest one was a huge framed poster that hung over his fireplace. It was a blow-up of the shot I'd seen in the guidebook: that still from the film of the sasquatch, with the monster looking over his shoulder, back at the cameraman. It was kind of blurry at that size, and very spooky looking. I stared at it.

"So," said Cosmos with a deep smile, bringing me out of my trance, "you know Walter Middy?"

"I'm...I'm his great-nephew."

"Well, you're a lucky man."

Huh?

"When old Walter first moved to these parts last year he came to us on the town council with an idea for bringing homeless Vancouver kids out here for a day at the beach. We thought it was a great idea, but too expensive. That was when he took out his chequebook. He paid every dime."

Alice and I looked at each other.

"You young folks are interested in the great ape, eh?"

It was almost shocking to hear him say that. It made me realize what I was doing. Me, once freaked out about the Reptile and monsters under my bed, and now I was sitting here with a real live sasquatch expert, interested.

"Do you really think it exists?" asked Alice.

"Yes! And I'll show you why," cried Cosmos as he leapt to his feet like a giant roused to action. He loped about two steps down his hallway to a closet, dug around inside for a while, and then came back. He was holding two huge chunks of plaster in his hands.

"This is why."

He set the plaster casts down, one on my lap, the other on Alice's. They were big feet.

"These are footprints, one made deep in the woods of the park, the other northeast of here near a place called Hell's Gate in the Fraser Canyon Valley. I made one pair, the renowned Professor Binderbugle the other."

"Footprints of what?" I asked.

"A sasquatch!"

They were massive. They covered both of my legs and then some. I could see each of the toes, almost humanlike. The big one stuck out a bit to the side. Could these be real? This thing would be a giant! A hairy giant *really* living in the woods of British Columbia?

Cosmos Greene started talking very fast.

"There are hundreds of footprint casts like these of sasquatches! And there have been thousands of sightings! Are *all* those witnesses simply hoax creators? Are they all liars? Gosh, the sightings go back to pre-colonial days. Indigenous people have talked about it for centuries. Did you know that when the Hudson's Bay Company established a post here in 1846, the inspector saw *many* of them? And they've been spotted right up to this decade. Science needs to deal with this subject seriously. If not with the existence of the sasquatch, then with the fact that so many people claim to have seen it. Are they delusional? And if they are, what does *that* mean? Why do people see monsters in the BC woods all the time? Why do they see them in the Himalayas of Asia?"

"Have you ever seen one, Mr. Greene?" inquired Alice.

"No," he said, almost sadly, slowing down for a breath. "I never have. But I've spoken to many witnesses and I've seen many, many actual footprints on the ground. *Something* is making those tracks and something is either causing people to *say* they've seen sasquatches...or they *are* seeing them!"

The scary thing about what he was saying was that it made some sense.

"It's an ape! A gigantic ape!" he bellowed.

"Pardon me?"

"Every sighting confirms it. Read descriptions of apes in the wild and then examine sasquatch sightings, and you'll see what I mean. Apes have an awful smell, you know. Many folks who have seen sasquatches report an overpowering odour in the air. They have a hard time describing it, but nine out of ten of them talk about it. There are places where they call it the skunk ape. Folks who have never seen an ape in their lives report all sorts of apelike characteristics, like chest thumping, rock throwing, and displaying and grimacing. It's *very* curious."

He started thumping himself on the chest.

"Where do people see them nowadays?"

He stopped.

"Everywhere, really. But mostly in the west: in

California, Oregon, Alberta, and British Columbia. And around here, of course!"

"Where here?"

"Why, are you planning a hunt?" He laughed long and loud, like a donkey braying.

"Of course not," I said, trying to be heard between the brays.

"Oh, they've been seen all around Harrison Lake," replied Cosmos, coming down to earth, "near the water, north, south, east, and west."

"In the park?" wondered Alice.

"Sure."

"Close by?" I asked.

"Absolutely."

IT TURNED OUT TO BE AN AMAZING VISIT. It lasted for more than an hour. At one point Cosmos's wife came out to say hello. She had a tray of cookies and some big tumblers of fruit juice. She sat still and listened, as if she deeply believed everything her husband was saying. It was kind of freaky. Alice and I kept glancing over at each other, raising our eyebrows. When we left, they saw us out at the door.

"You should ask your uncle about this."

"Why?"

"I have the feeling…he's seen one."

WE WALKED ALONG THE BEACH, talking. What Cosmos Greene had said about my uncle was weird enough. But he had filled our heads with some other pretty bizarre ideas too. He had actually started laying out ways to get close to a sasquatch. He said maybe some raw meat, like dead rats, left in a well-hidden place in the woods, visible from a hiding spot, might do the trick. He told us that searchers have to treat it like an animal, get upwind from it, be absolutely quiet, track it if they find footprints, that sort of thing. And, of course, he said they have to be alert for smells. Close up, he claimed, the odour is like rotting meat. I couldn't believe he was serious. Check out the sasquatch? Maybe people should try for the Easter Bunny while they're at it.

But the way Alice was talking, it didn't sound like she thought any of this was even remotely like a fantasy egg hunt. She said she was "blown away" by Uncle Walter and Cosmos Greene, that they were the only adults she'd ever met who weren't boring. And she was fired up with everything we had heard about the sasquatch. She was almost jumping up and down like a little kid.

"What if we saw one? Can you imagine?" she asked.

"Come on, Alice," I sneered, but I was wondering the same thing.

"Cosmos thinks your uncle's seen it!"

"He's just guessing."

"What if Walter *is* holding something back? What if he really did see something? Could he just let it go? A man like him? I mean, why's he here?" she said.

"He just wants to live a quiet life."

"Oh, yes, in sleepy Harrison Hot Springs, the home of the sasquatch."

"I don't know, Alice."

But at that instant, an image came into my mind that really made me wonder. I could see the boot tray on Uncle Walter's balcony...and I remembered him walking away from us on the boardwalk. *He was always wearing hiking boots.* Why? Were they good golf wear, or perfect for the beach? And why were they so often muddy? *Was he doing something out in the forest?*

"His boots. Right?" said Alice, smiling at me. It was like she'd been inside my head. It startled me.

"Yeah," I said.

"He's holding something back, Dylan, and you know it."

"Maybe," I replied. But I was sure now that deep inside my uncle a whole world was waiting for me, a world of excitement...if I could only lose my fear.

"There's one way to find out," said Alice firmly.

"How's that?"

"Follow him."

"Follow him?"

"Yeah...stake him out."

And that was how I came to be out of bed by five o'clock in the morning the following day, and then outside under the moonlit sky before the sun rose over the mountains of Sasquatch Provincial Park. I couldn't believe I was doing it. It seemed like a dream.

7

THE SECRET HIDEOUT

Five o'clock in the morning isn't my time of day. But there I was, walking along the boardwalk, rubbing my eyes, the skies dark above me. My body was still asleep but my brain was wide awake. I kept looking behind me and around each corner. The whole place was spooky. The mountains seemed to move, like huge faces looming over the water. And the lake itself was a big, black piece of glass just sitting there in silence. Everything was too dark and too quiet. I almost ran towards Walter's condo.

I could see Alice in the distance. You could have fired a cannonball down the Esplanade and not touched a living soul: except her.

She had stepped out onto the street so I could see her. Then she moved back into the shadows. As I approached, I detected her glued against the outside wall of Walter's building, dressed in dark clothes. Before we could even say hello, a glow flashed out over the street, four storeys up.

Uncle Walter's lights were coming on!

"You see!" whispered Alice excitedly.

Fifteen minutes later we heard a nearby garage door rise and a weird-looking vehicle lumbered out. I learned later that it was called a Hummer. They're these Jeeps that almost look like tanks, very wide and able to go just about anywhere. But, as I would soon find out, this one could go places even your average Hummer couldn't.

Most of these things are apparently green, sometimes even camouflage colours. This model was black and white...painted up like a chessboard. My mouth dropped open. Only someone with a pretty wild imagination would drive something like this.

Its door opened and out stepped Uncle Walter. He had his hiking boots on. He opened the rear door of the vehicle and peered in for a while, rummaging around in a huge trunk that covered the whole length of the back seat. Something must have been missing, because after a while he stepped back, moved quickly up the walkway, and disappeared through the front door of the condo. We were still pinned against the wall. We could see the trunk sitting in the Hummer, the rear door wide open.

Suddenly, Alice made for it. I dashed after her. We leapt up. The trunk had no lid on it, so we just ducked inside and made ourselves as small and quiet as possible. There were all kinds of tools under us and I was trying not to be too cozy with Alice, so it was pretty uncomfortable. She didn't seem nearly as worried about getting close. A minute later we heard Walter walking back to the street. As he came towards us we flattened ourselves against each other, but he didn't see us. He threw something into the trunk without looking. It landed on my gut and nearly knocked the wind out of me: his binoculars. He slammed the door shut, shuffled around to the driver's seat, got in and pulled away.

Going against parental-unit advice was always a bad idea, and here I was doing it as big time as I possibly could. But I was taking on something exciting again too, something a bit scary—and actually enjoying it.

I kept my eyes and ears wide open. Walter plugged his iPod in and cranked up the volume. It was that band, Jefferson Airplane, again, and that weird song "White Rabbit." I could make out more of the words:

about chasing something through a strange land and a giant caterpillar that smoked. Now *that* sounded druggie to me.

We headed off down the Esplanade, going the opposite direction from the resort. Every now and then Alice or I would cautiously peek out over the top of the trunk and look out through the rear windows. The Hummer zoomed past the Bungalow Motel and its cabins at the far end of town and sped along the road by the lake that led into Sasquatch Provincial Park. Why was Walter going there?

At first the road was paved, winding its way along the east end of the water and slowly climbing. Then it curved directly into the camping areas. It turned to gravel, then to dirt, and became snakelike and narrow. We seemed to go past every possible entrance to picnic areas and the park's two lakes, Hicks and Deer. Finally, we came to a dead end. Walter brought his vehicle to a stop. There was no one around.

He got out.

We scrunched down as low as we could. We could hear his feet crunching pine needles and leaves on the ground. A couple of times, I caught sight of his eyes as he moved around the Hummer. He looked happier than usual. The cool morning air was damp and thick, the sun was rising, and you could hear all sorts of birds. One sounded like a crow, a big one. It was louder than all the rest. When it cawed, Uncle Walter stopped what he was doing, looked up, and waved. Was he motioning to a bird? This was getting weird. Walter moved around the vehicle again, and leaned way down. It sounded like he was pressing buttons or something near the wheels. The whole thing kind of shuddered like an airplane does when its landing gear comes up. Then it really shook. We were thrown around inside the trunk, the tools shifting beneath us like we were lying on marbles. What was he doing? What *in the world* was he doing?

Walter got back up into his driver's seat. I peeked over the edge of the trunk again. We were off the road and at the very edge of the forest. I lifted my head higher, stuck it slightly out the lowered window, and quickly glanced down at the wheels. They were gone! Replaced by bulldozer tracks! I tucked my head back in and tried to mouth the words to Alice, but she looked at me in confusion, like I was either speaking Vulcan or she couldn't believe what I was trying to say. Walter stepped on the gas.

He drove right into the woods!

It was amazing. He just gunned the engine and we went right in, almost through the trees it seemed. In seconds it felt like we were inside some sort of massive room, with a floor of thick moss and stumps. Trees were everywhere, practically blurring together as they rose straight up into a huge, cathedral ceiling of green leaves and pine needles. Walter roared the Hummer forward, bounding up and down along an invisible road. We held on, our palms pressed against the walls of the trunk, our faces grimacing as we stared up at the giant British Columbia wooded wonderland. Light shone through our forest ceiling in shafts like laser beams from outer space.

Every now and then I peeked out. I kept seeing things in the maze of trees: rabbits rushing by as if late for something, brightly coloured birds swooping past, furry animals that looked like beavers and bigger ones that might have even been bear cubs. And every now and then I could have sworn I saw things that were taller and on two legs like human beings running through the green lit trees. We were in some other reality.

After about fifteen minutes of crashing forward we were deep into the forest, far away from civilization. Then, suddenly, we stopped. It didn't seem any different here than any other spot we'd passed since entering the forest, but Walter jumped out like he had arrived at something. Alice and I shifted uncomfortably in the trunk. Seconds later he came around to the back of the vehicle. Then he opened the door. He reached into the trunk. Glancing up, I saw his face, but it was turned away, looking up into the sky for something. I gently handed him the binoculars. He grabbed them absent-mindedly and shut the back door.

We heard him trudging away from us, his footsteps getting fainter. We sat up, our eyes just over the lip of the trunk, and saw how deep in the forest we really were, among a million trees. Then we caught sight of Walter about thirty metres away, bending over a big stump. As we watched, he pulled it up by the roots with a grunt... and disappeared under the ground.

Then the stump seemed to move back into place like magic.

We looked at each other. *What had just happened?* Slowly we got out of the trunk, jumped down, and tiptoed over to the spot where Walter had vanished.

Alice pulled on the stump. It lifted up in her hands with ease. She peered down into the black hole underneath, so dark we couldn't see more than a metre into it. We both kept staring, speechless. We couldn't believe it. But when I lifted my eyes to meet Alice's, a determined expression was beginning to spread across her face. "Ready or not," she said and stepped into the hole. Instantly she vanished downward. Dazed, I felt around near the opening. Then I stuck my head partway inside. I could smell the earth. But Alice was gone!

So. I could either stay here alone, deep in the woods with the bears and the wolves and the sasquatch, or I could follow Walter and Alice down this stump hole. I listened to the sounds of the forest for a second. Now they were eerie. I sat down on the edge of the hole, dangling my feet in. Then I let myself drop.

It felt like I fell for about half an hour, but it was probably a few seconds. It went from darkness and dirt-dampness to light and I made an abrupt but soft landing. I was sitting on a thick air bag, like a stuntperson might use to break a fall off a building; like the human cannonball uses in the circus. Alice was right beside me, gaping at her surroundings as if her eyes might pop out of her head. Then I saw Uncle Walter. He was standing above us, staring at me, his mouth wide open.

"You...you followed me?" he said, looking betrayed.

"What is this?" I gasped, getting to my feet, stunned, looking around. I felt like shaking my head to wake myself up. It was as if I'd fallen into a dream.

Right beside us was an underground room. It was a rough rectangle, nearly five metres long, with a ceiling almost three metres high. Someone had put up dry wall and painted it. There was a stove, a sink...

and a TV, with an aerial that went straight up into the ground above. In the cupboards I could see chips and soft drinks and candies. I saw an electrical cord on the wooden floor, heading off down a narrow hallway. On the walls were pictures from Walter's circus days and one of the sasquatch.

"It's...it's my place..." said Walter. "You...forgot to close the door."

He picked up a big pole with a hook on the end that was lying on the ground next to the air bag. Then he stuck it up the hole, telescoped it upward, hooked onto something, and pulled the lid, or the stump, back on top. Immediately, the sounds of the forest, a bit distant anyway, were totally shut out. It was perfectly silent inside.

"You learn to be inventive in the circus. I used to build all sorts of things. This is all I have left of my past," said Walter. "Everything about my life is normal now, except this. This is where I come to get away. I wish you hadn't followed me." He paused, looking upset. "What will your parents think? They'll be worried sick."

There was a sudden sound up above us in the direction of the stump. Someone, or something, was rapping on the "door." Alice and I both sat bolt upright. How could anyone have followed us?

Uncle Walter looked remarkably calm. In fact, he actually smiled.

"Just a minute. Just a minute!" he cackled. With that, he shoved the pole back up the hole and forced open the hatch. Instantly we heard a raspy cawing and the sound of big wings flapping, and down into the space came a huge, black bird. Alice and I ducked and held our arms over our scalps, foreheads down on the air bag. But all we heard were more swooping wings, strange bird words, and Uncle Walter's fatherly voice. I peeked out through my fingers with one eye.

"Yes, yes, baby, I forgot you, didn't I?" he cooed, his head bobbing up and down as he followed the dark, flying wonder. "'Grim, ungainly, ghastly, gaunt, and ominous bird of yore'…come here."

He held out his arm and the big raven landed lightly. "Lady and gentleman, may I present the ultimate trickster, Mr. Poe." It was larger than Uncle Walter's head.

"Poe!" said the raven.

"He comes from the Queen Charlotte Islands. My last wife, my dear late wife, bought him years ago just before I retired, from a Haida gentleman who had trained him. He would have been wonderful for the circus, but I like him better the way he is. Wild."

"Wild!" said the raven.

"Do you know that ravens are the smartest birds in existence? They can be taught to talk better than any parrot. Black and tricky and smart and legendary: that's the way I like my little flying machines. One can never have too many clever friends when one is looking around out here."

"Sassss—squash!" cried the raven.

"That's sas-*squatch*, Poe. Sas-*squatch!*"

"Sassss—squash! "

"He's such a comedian."

I glanced down the narrow hallway, wondering where it led. Uncle Walter noticed.

"You're right, Dylan. It leads that way. Want to see it?" And with that he turned towards the passageway and began walking down it, with more spring in his step than I'd ever seen. Alice leapt to her feet and followed. She was loving everything she was seeing. Her eyes were shining. I scrambled after them. Poe jumped up onto one of Walter's shoulders and expertly turned around. From there, he watched us. His eyeballs turned white and then back to black. He seemed to smile.

"Ki-ids!" he cried.

There was lots of light in the hallway at first and I could see the electrical cord running along on the floor. But we hadn't gone very far before our passage got darker and much narrower. We were crouching as we walked…and I was starting to freak out: tunnels give me the creeps—they make me feel like I can't breathe. But soon, things got lighter and I could hear footsteps on wood up ahead, as if Walter was climbing stairs. In seconds, I reached them too. They went straight up, in a steep, narrow, spiral staircase.

I started climbing, Walter's and Alice's steps sounding directly above me. As the stairs wound around, we just kept going up and up. We were in some sort of tube, lit by thousands of little holes. It seemed as if we were above ground again. I noticed the electrical cord taped to the boards and going upward with us. Then I saw a bigger hole up ahead, with more light shining through. When I reached it, I pressed my face to it and looked out. We weren't just above ground: we were way above it! I almost fell back down the stairs. It was like peering over the edge of a tall building. I could smell something like pine needles. Looking out and straight down, I saw bark and more bark. We were in a huge tree! And we were climbing to the top of it, from the *inside!*

Maybe Walter had built a fake tree tower around a staircase? Maybe I was really losing my mind?

"Uh, Uncle Walter, where are we *now?*"

"You'll see," he said. "We're almost at the peak."

Three minutes later the staircase ascended into what looked like someone's living room: a very cool living room, at least ten metres long and half of that wide. Alice did a little swirl and sort of floated across the wooden floor in a dance with herself, her head pointed straight up and glowing with excitement. I looked up too and saw a roof filled with glass and beyond it blue sky. I realized that the glass part was a bunch of solar panels—the power source—just like a friend's house back in Toronto. There were big windows all around. I walked over to one of them and looked out. I couldn't believe it. We were *way* up in the air, almost in the sky, at the top of some of the tallest trees in the forest. And the trees here were gigantic. We were in Uncle Walter Middy's tree fort...his secret hideout.

It was so amazing that it made me smile. And I didn't care how he'd done it. I suddenly felt truly happy for the first time since we'd left Alberta. Alice and I just walked around the room staring at the place. There were all kinds of illustrations and posters on the walls. The biggest one was of a guy I recognized. John Lennon, one of The Beatles, from the 1960s. It was a strange picture. He was sitting in a field of big red strawberries beneath a sky of diamonds, and underneath him was the word IMAGINE.

Uncle Walter had moved over to one of the largest windows and was standing there, looking out into the forest with his binoculars. Poe pushed off from his shoulder, pulled open a latch on a window with his beak, and flew out. We could see him dash straight up into the blue, becoming a speck.

"Uh, Mr. Middy?" asked Alice.

He lowered the binoculars. "Yes?"

"What *is* this place, really?"

"You can see for miles and miles from here, can't you?"

"Better to see *him*?"

"I'm not sure what you mean," he said. "I come here to be alone: to think. We're out of the park, by the way, a good three or four kilometres beyond the boundary." He paused. "About twenty years ago someone found footprints right under this tree fort, heading northeast. *Big* footprints. Or so he said. When I came to investigate the spot, I loved it. So, I built this place. But that was years ago, before I even moved here permanently, when I believed in nonsense, before I started making sense out of my life. It was childish, I guess. I try not to come here too often."

"Are we, uh, searching for him today?" I inquired, finding it difficult to believe that I was actually asking that question.

"I'm not sure what you mean," repeated Walter, gazing through the binoculars again.

"Why don't we go into the forest and you can show us where those old footprints were?" Alice asked.

"That wouldn't make you a bad person," I kidded him.

Walter set the binoculars down abruptly, like he'd had enough. "I have to get you both back. You're my responsibility."

Within minutes he had guided us back down the tree, into the underground room, and back up and out the stump. Then he herded us into the Hummer and roared back through the forest. As we neared the spot where he'd entered the woods, we saw some figures moving towards us through the trees. *What was this?*

It was two people, struggling to get their footing as they made their way over the tough undergrowth. From a distance, I thought I recognized the way they walked. A minute later, I knew I did. It was Mom and Dad. And man, were they ticked off.

How'd they find out where we were?

"So, you've changed, have you!" shouted Dad as Walter climbed down from the Hummer and helped Alice and me out.

"You have every right to be angry," said Walter quietly. "I'm sorry.

"Sorry isn't good enough. Not when my son's involved!" cried Mom. "Aren't there grizzly bears around here?"

"Yes," said Walter, "I'm sorry."

"That's a big word with you these days, isn't it?" Why didn't he just tell the truth? It was my fault, and Alice's!

"Mom, it isn't his faul—"

"Quiet, Dylan!" snapped Dad. "Someone saw you, Walter, driving off at an ungodly hour this morning, heading this way. Otherwise, we might never have found you.

"We were coming back, Dad!"

"I told you to hold your tongue!"

I stopped talking. Mom and Dad weren't being rational.

"What's out here, anyway, Walter?"

"Nothing."

"Nothing? A child's response! Perfect! What are you looking for...the sasquatch?"

"No, John. Just experiencing nature."

"In that thing?" Dad pointed at the Hummer. "Dylan, young lady, you're coming with us. Walter, you'll be driving that tank alone. And..." He paused and gave Walter a long look. "We've seen the last of each other."

"Of course," replied Walter weakly. "Goodbye, Dylan. Alice."

I felt a pang of sadness as I watched Walter's shoulders sag. He turned his back and walked away.

Was he just giving up? Why didn't he fight for himself? All that amazing spirit he'd had as a kid was gone. I wanted to scream at my parents that it wasn't his fault. But I didn't. I joined them and started trudging out of the forest. Maybe I'd lost my spirit, too, for good.

On our way out we saw someone Alice thought we'd been seeing entirely too much of: Lance Bennett. He was standing at the edge of the forest where we'd entered, holding a shotgun, still in its case.

Lance? *Was he the guy who saw the Hummer leaving this morning?*

"Thanks," said Dad as he walked past him.

"No problem. I'm always an early riser. Just happened to be looking out the window."

Alice glared at him.

"What's the gun for?" I asked.

"Never know what you might find out here, Dylan," he intoned. "Might bag me a sasquatch."

8

SOMEBODY TO LOVE

They didn't start yelling until after we dropped Alice off at Carol's rooms and made our way up to our own suite.

"Get in here!" shouted Dad.

They very rarely yell at me. They claim not to believe in it. But I didn't mind. It really made me feel like they cared. I guess they were pretty worried about me. They didn't even give me much chance to explain. That was unusual too. The Reptile, and now this: they were pretty freaked out.

But after about a ten-minute lecture, things started to get calmer. Mom was leading the way in the calming-down department.

"Honey, we don't think you should see Uncle Walter again."

"You make it sound like we're dating or something."

"Don't hang out with him then, smart guy!" snapped Dad.

"Why?"

"Why? How can you ask me that? You could have been killed by a grizzly, or God knows what. Thank goodness for this Lance Bennett chap."

"Uncle Walter wouldn't have put us in any danger. It was our fault anyway, like I told you. He took us back just after he found us."

"Yeah, right."

"You should see what he has out there."

"I don't want to know," said Mom, her voice rising a little. "He's been crazy and irresponsible since the day he was born."

"But maybe you've never *really* tried to get to know him."

"Oh, I know him, young man."

"He wouldn't hurt a flea."

"Ask his dead wife!" Dad snapped.

There was silence for a second. It seemed as though the air had just been sucked out of the room. I looked at both of them and they looked back. What were they talking about?

Mom put her arm around me. "Someday I'll tell you all about it. But not now. You had a horrible time last week. You need to take it easy. It was a mistake to make up with Uncle Walter. A leopard never changes its spots."

"Mom, I don't want to…retreat…anymore. I know that now. I want to have *fun* again. Don't you see? That's what I really need. I think that's what Uncle Walter needs, too."

Mom sighed. Then she spoke quietly. "If you want to have fun, Dylan, go swimming, relax in the hot springs. Don't go out alone into a BC rainforest filled with who knows what!" Then she paused and tried to lighten things up. "Don't you know that's sasquatch country?"

I didn't laugh, so there was silence for a few seconds. Then they both turned away to get changed. Their clothes were pretty muddy.

"Do you think there's any chance it exists?" I asked them.

They stopped at exactly the same time, and sighed together. Mom turned around.

"Come on, Dylan, we've been through this. I was making a joke."

"You don't think it's possible? Hundreds of people say they've seen it. And they've found lots of footprints. Are all those people lying; are all those footprints fake?"

"Almost anything's possible," said Dad curtly, "but not that."

"Why?"

"I don't want to talk about it anymore. Why are you bringing this up again?"

"Do you really believe that almost anything's possible, Dad?"

He never answered that one. By then he was shaking his head in Mom's direction. They didn't know what the heck to do with me. Ground me? While I was supposed to be on vacation recovering from what I'd been through in Alberta? I don't think so.

"Are you okay?" asked Mom very quietly a few minutes later, looking deeply into my face. *I* didn't answer that one.

I had the weirdest dream that night. It felt like I had been dreaming in my dream and then woke up. All I saw was blue sky out a car window.

THE NEXT FEW DAYS were much quieter. Mom and Dad kept me away from Uncle Walter's condo and we did some family things. We went water skiing, did lots of swimming, hung out in the hot springs and even tried golfing, which is a bit of a doofus sport as far as I'm concerned.

I saw Alice a few times, and even introduced Mom and Dad to Carol. Alice and I tried out the Blaster Bumper Boat rides: you bomb around smashing into other boats and firing off big water rifles. We formed a pretty good team. She loved to get her hands on the gun and really got into trying to win. Any time we got shot, she was pretty upset. We also tried these amazing ten-person banana tube rides where you get towed across the lake at mega-speed by a powerboat. You get totally soaked and sometimes bounced right into Harrison Lake. Alice always wanted us to sit close together, to help us stay on, she said. She kind of leaned on me when we went around corners, and fell on top of me quite a few times.

She often asked about Uncle Walter. What was there to say? I told her I wasn't allowed to see him. She didn't understand. "Allowed?" she asked, as if that were a Martian word. But Walter had vanished from the beaches anyway, like a magician.

Mom said Alice seemed "like a nice girl, despite that thing in her belly button." She and Dad were invited to spend a day on the Tweedledum and Tweedledee yacht.

They got along okay with Lance and Carol, though I could tell they really weren't my parents' type. Alice rolled her eyes when Carol appeared on deck in a new, sparkling gold bikini. She could hardly wait to get me away from them all. Late in the afternoon, she grabbed my hand and whipped me around to the back of the boat. Then she shoved me into the water. We swam back to the beach together and lay down on the sand.

"I hate her."

"You hate your mom?"

"Like, totally."

"My mom and dad are kind of goofy, I guess, sometimes, but—"

"Your parents aren't so bad."

"They aren't?"

"No. At least your dad's around. I see mine about once a month. He and Carol split up when I was six. He's very busy, too. Places to go and people to meet, you know. I can still remember playing with them, both of them...when I was a little kid. Now he's never around, and she's always out, working for some company or another. All that matters to her is money. She's a fake."

Alice Carr was a bit like someone in the novels that my buds and I were forced to read at school, where the characters always come from dysfunctional families, or have some horrible problem the authors have drummed up. Not that Alice was a moaner. She just genuinely didn't seem happy.

"I want something, Dylan."

Uh-oh. I didn't like that comment. Then she reached out and held my hand.

For some stupid reason, I pulled away.

"Hand it over, goof," she laughed, and grabbed my hand again. "I was just going to look at your life line!"

She took my hand and turned it palm-up. Her hands were awfully soft and my heart started beating faster. What a doink!

"This line," she said, tracing her finger along the curving mark bordering my thumb, "is wild!" Her finger made my hand ticklish. "What an imagination you've got, Dylan! No wonder you're interested in the sasquatch!"

It looked like a normal line to me.

"Look at mine," she said. "Let's compare."

She held her hand, a bit smaller than mine and tipped with bright red polish on her nails and a couple of rings on her fingers, so that her palm pressed against my palm. Then she pulled it back.

"See, I have a really curvy line of imagination too. But check this one out."

She pointed to a crease going straight across her hand. It looked deeply cut.

"This is the desire line. That means I have lots of desire about everything."

Uh-oh again. I wanted to be somewhere else. I started looking out to the water to see if our parents were floating back in. And actually, they were. The yacht was easing towards the dock.

"I want people to have time for each other and be interested in each other," continued Alice. "I like that song that your uncle plays, that old one about needing somebody to love."

I was hoping she wasn't going to quote it to me.

"I'm so *sick* of adult problems. I just want to be a kid again. I *really* do. Don't you?"

"Uh, yeah. Look, the yacht is docking."

"I just want to have fun."

I stood up. Alice sat there for a few seconds then she stood too, laughed, and gave me a shove.

"You're such a suck, Maples."

"What?"

When I turned and looked at her, her bright blue eyes were smiling at me and her black hair was hanging down, wet and sandy around her tanned face. She had this look like a real friend would have, like somebody who's *really* interested in you, and in what makes you tick. I kind of liked that look and found it sort of creepy at the same time.

"I'd like to know what you're thinking sometimes." She laughed, and shoved me again.

"Not much," I offered. "Let's go see the units."

I walked towards the yacht and she didn't follow for a while. But by the time I got to the dock she was there, right beside me, like I guess I'd hoped.

"Dylan Maples and Alice Carr! What a pleasure to be met here at the edge of the Riviera by such a worldly couple!"

It was Lance Bennett. What a doorknob. He actually had a captain's hat on. He leapt out of the boat onto the dock and began tying things up. Mom and Dad came down, too, not looking too comfortable around their new friends, but smiling at me. Then Lance helped Carol off, like she was a princess or something. He also helped her into this pink, silky-looking robe thing that she wrapped around herself. The letters "T & T" were emblazoned on it, and the whole thing looked like an expensive dress.

"How embarrassing," whispered Alice. We started to walk away.

"Stay. Stay!" cried Lance. "I have something I want you to see."

In minutes he had marched us all to a place near the boardwalk off the esplanade. The beach was on one side, the town on the other. A big truck was sitting there with a wrecking ball hanging down from a crane. It loomed over about ten old houses. Reporters, cameras, and microphones were formed into a little semicircle in front of a podium. A crowd was gathering, looking curious, and some munchies had been laid out on tables nearby.

What was this all about? What was going on?

As we approached, Lance swept off his hat and his sailor's jacket, revealing just a T-shirt that was supposed to look ordinary, but was one of those designer shirts that cost the big bucks. I noticed he was wearing jeans, blue ones that were faded just perfectly. Carol was slipping on a pair of high heels to wear under that robe-turned-dress thing she had on. She was also checking her face in a make-up mirror and putting on some bright red lipstick. Then she started nodding to the reporters, shaking people's hands, thanking them for coming.

"Here she goes," said Alice with a sigh, "Ms. PR, on the job."

Lance stepped up to the microphone. A silver shovel leaned against his podium.

"Welcome," he said with a huge smile on his face, "to the newest phase of the Tweedledum and Tweedledee healthy candy empire: the stores that feed the imagination. We have arrived in Harrison Hot Springs at stunning Harrison Lake, home of Canada's most beautiful resort and—" he winked at me, "—the sasquatch monster."

There was scattered laughter from the crowd. Mom and Dad grinned with the others.

Then Lance went on to describe this huge new store and spa that he was going to build on the spot where they were about to wreck these old houses. Carol slowly moved up towards the podium until she was standing almost beside him, smiling at everyone. Before long he reached for the silver shovel. This was the sort of goofy thing that adults do when they're about to put up a new building. The mayor of the town and the owner and other dignitaries pretend they're about to begin building the place right there all by themselves by putting a shovel into the ground and posing for pictures. Of course, people like that wouldn't know how to build an outhouse. But this time, Lance stopped just before they snapped the shots.

"Ladies and gentlemen, before we do the requisite posing in this fabulous town of the wilderness legend, may I introduce…Tweedledum and Tweedledee!"

With that, a long limousine pulled up and the doors swung open. Out of each side came the two largest human beings I had ever seen. They looked like they were well over six feet tall and weighed a thousand pounds between them. And they were almost naked— big, fat, muscular...*sumo wrestlers*—dressed in the little diaper-type things those guys wear.

"3-D," said Alice into my ear.

The crowd oohed and aahed a bit, some even giggled. The sumo wrestlers seemed to understand. They even hammed it up a bit. They posed for pictures, then Lance directed the crowd to the food and the interviews began. Things were about to get boring. There was no way Alice and I were hanging around for this part.

So, we snuck away and went looking for Uncle Walter. We knew we weren't supposed to, but it was a perfect opportunity. The adults were so into what they were doing, they didn't even notice. It seemed to me there'd be no harm in just talking to him for a while.

We slipped into his condominium building when someone else opened the front entrance. We even got by the second set of doors and up the elevator to his apartment. Standing there, knocking, was Cosmos Greene.

"Oh," he said, turning to us, "how are you youngsters?" He seemed a bit distracted.

"I don't think he's there," I said.

"Yes," replied Greene, "I think you're right." He paused. "Well, I must be going."

"Just dropping by to say hello?" asked Alice.

"Well, yes. Sort of."

"Sort of?" I asked.

Cosmos hesitated. "I'll tell you why I'm here, if you promise not to tell anyone else."

We nodded.

"There's been a sighting."

"A sighting?"

"A sasquatch sighting."

He could see the excitement come into our faces. "Now, don't get all fired up, youngsters. We have many reports. Hundreds. Most of them are hoaxes. Though this one sounds pretty good. From a couple of hunters."

"But why are you here? What does this have to do with my uncle Walter?"

"Well," said Cosmos, hesitating again. "He...usually comes with me."

"He does?" asked Alice.

Images of those muddy boots re-entered my mind.

"He knows more about the sasquatch than anyone other than myself," laughed Cosmos. We didn't laugh. We were just staring at him. "He learned a great deal about it when he was in showbiz and he's just fascinated by it. Started coming here long ago looking for one. Mysteries and adventures, you know, that's circus stuff. And I told you...I think he saw one. But for some reason, he won't say anything about it. I just have this feeling though...."

He seemed lost in thought for a few seconds.

"Are you investigating it now?" asked Alice.

"Yes." He moved off down the hallway.

"Can we come?"

"No, no. That wouldn't be right."

He could see our disappointment. But Alice wasn't giving up so easily. "Where was the sighting?" she blurted out.

"Just off the main park road into the woods past the boundary, where hunting is allowed." He was near the end of the hall. "I have to be going. Nice to see you again."

We stood still outside Walter's door and watched Cosmos disappear around the corner. Then we looked at each other.

"Let's go," we said at the same time.

THERE'S A SHUTTLE BUS that takes campers up to Sasquatch Provincial Park. It goes every hour during the day. We were in luck. When we got there it was ten minutes from takeoff. Soon we were winding our way back up the main park road. The bus kept stopping at various campsites, letting off people who carried grocery bags towards trailers. There was no sign of Greene. Then, deep into the park, before the bus turned around to head back to town, we saw a car pulled off to the side. We checked out the licence plate, COSMOS, it read. Moments later we were standing on the road, eyeing a fresh path that led into the woods.

9

ON THE TRAIL

As we entered the forest I glanced over at Alice. She had this look on her face like she was ready to fly to the moon. She caught my eye and gave me a smile that I'd never seen before. She was incredibly happy. We raced into the woods, the ferns whipping against our pant legs.

Before long we heard voices. We froze. Then we began moving much slower and quieter. It was hard not to make the leaves crunch under our feet. With every step we were afraid we'd be heard.

"About here?" asked one of the voices.

It was Cosmos Greene.

"Yes," said another.

"Yeah, I'd say that's right," added a third.

As we moved cautiously forward we saw them through the trees about thirty metres away. Greene and the two hunters, dressed in their bright orange vests, looking a little scared.

The old man seemed to sense something and turned to look back in our direction. We ducked down like we'd been shot. He stood very still and listened. When he turned around again, we moved forward on our hands and knees. Soon we could almost hear them breathing.

"And where was the creature, Mr. Barrett?"

"That direction." Barrett pointed.

"Correct, Mr. Vander Zalm?"

"Correct."

They had come to a slight opening in the woods. Fifty metres away the trees got thicker again. They all stood very still for a while. There was silence.

"Yeah, it was over there, all right," mumbled Barrett, his eyes opening wide as he looked out across the clearing.

"It didn't see us. I don't think. We left, really fast."

"Maybe we were seeing things? Maybe…maybe we should go?"

"Let me take a look," whispered Cosmos, putting a reassuring arm on Barrett. The men were all glancing around now, watching for any movement in the forest, listening for strange sounds. Cosmos examined the trees. Slowly they inched their way in the direction Barrett said the sasquatch had been. As Cosmos got closer, he lowered his head, examining the ground. Then he stopped.

"Oh…my…God," we heard him say.

Alice and I rose a little, straining to see what he was looking down at. The men rushed over to where he was crouching.

"Here's another one," he said, standing up and moving forward. "And another. And another." He walked bent at the waist, his eyes on the ground, still moving in the direction the creature had been spotted.

When he was ten metres farther, Alice and I took a chance. We scurried through the brush towards the spot where Cosmos had first bent over and threw ourselves on the ground. We looked down, our faces a toadstool's height from the dirt.

The footprint was unmistakable. It was about half a metre long, a lot like the one Cosmos had made his plaster cast of. Most impressively, it was sunk down into the earth.

"Look at the depth," we heard Cosmos loudly whisper up ahead of us. I peeked up through the ferns and saw his eyes gazing down, all ablaze.

I knew what he meant. At his house, he had told us that many sasquatch footprints were hoaxes, just people trying to have a good time with big fake feet, running around making imprints to see if others would believe they were on the trail of a sasquatch. But these passed the test instantly. They sank several centimetres into the ground, ground that wasn't soft and was scattered with Douglas fir needles and leaves: the men's feet weren't even leaving a mark. These tracks had to be made by something big, very big, much bigger than any human being who had ever walked the earth.

We heard Cosmos click open a little tape measure and stick it into the print.

"I'd say that whatever made that weighed—about eight or nine hundred pounds."

"That's almost half a ton!" gasped Alice, right beside my ear.

"We should get out of here," cried Vander Zalm.

"And they keep going," said Cosmos, following the direction the toes were pointed in, "this way." He moved along in a crouch and we followed. There were more and more prints. Some were on muddy patches and incredibly clear—you could see five toe marks on each—real toes, not claws like a bear's tracks would have. And each print was separated from the other by more than a metre. That was something else Cosmos had said to look for: a sasquatch's stride was much greater than a human being's. Anybody faking these prints would have to be not only heavy, but able to run awfully fast to keep the marks far apart. That would have been virtually impossible.

"Put the guns away, boys," we heard Cosmos say quietly. He had stood up and stopped, as if he was readying himself for something.

The men hesitated. They looked at each other.

"I'll put the safety on," said Barrett, "but that's it. I'm keeping it in my hands."

"You didn't see this thing!" added Vander Zalm.

They clicked the safeties into position.

Cosmos turned and started walking faster. We scrambled to keep up, trying to stay low. We were stepping over fallen trunks and veering around stumps, still worried about the sound of leaves crunching beneath our feet. Then, without the men saying anything to each other, their pace picked up. Before long they were jogging. It was as if they could feel the sasquatch getting nearer. We began to move faster too.

The footprints remained fairly clear. They were on a straight line through the forest. Then we started to smell something very strong. I remembered what Cosmos had said about other people who had encountered the monster.

Man! Was I about to become a sasquatch witness?

The smell grew stronger. It was as if a pack of skunks had unloaded near us. Why did it smell like skunks?

Cosmos held up his hand and they all stopped. We froze too. Everything was silent except for five people breathing heavily. Then we heard a rustling in the forest up ahead.

THERE!

Something moved in the trees. It was at least a hundred metres away but we could tell it was big and black. It stood upright as it ran and looked far larger than a bear!

Vander Zalm and Barrett cried out.

We straightened up and raced forward, not caring who saw us now. We let loose and began to sprint. A rush of energy exploded inside me. I was scared, but I loved it. I felt like a kid again. Cosmos, who had come to a halt as the others roared forward, looked at us in disbelief as we surged past him. I noticed an old video camera in his hand. We glanced at him and then locked our eyes on the blur way out in front of us.

My heart was pounding. I felt like slapping myself in the face to see if I was dreaming. Here we were, chasing a sasquatch! Or something. It was so hard to believe it was really the monster itself.

But whatever was in those trees pulled away from us rapidly. It seemed incredibly athletic, leaping over fallen trunks, dodging through the trees. No bear could move like that. Before long it must have been half a kilometre away.

Far behind us, Cosmos Greene tore his binoculars off his neck in anger and hurled them into the woods towards us. They landed not far from our feet. I picked them up and turned them in the direction of our rapidly disappearing prey. Nothing. It was gone! But as I swept the lens across the trees, I noticed something else. I whipped them back.

A huge, dark figure was standing there in the woods! It was about thirty metres away, perfectly camouflaged in the trees, watching. *A second one!* I blinked my eyes and focused. It vanished.

I stood there for a moment, frantically adjusting and re-adjusting the lens, unable to believe my eyes, and unable to find the dark figure again. Then I started to run, in the direction I'd seen it.

"Alice, I think I—"

She ran after me. And there, on the ground, *I saw another footprint,* pointed towards the spot I'd seen the creature through the binoculars. *It was deeper than the others, much longer, and nearly twice as wide!*

But suddenly a strong hand gripped me by the arm. It was Cosmos. He was out of breath and looked angry.

"Do your parents know you're here?" he shouted.

"But I saw—"

"Do they?"

Barrett and Vander Zalm started calling out to him. They had stopped a long distance away, having made better time chasing the creature. But it was obvious now that whatever we were all pursuing wasn't going to be caught.

"Mr. Greene!" Vander Zalm was shouting. "It's gone!" He almost seemed relieved. He paced around a bit in the trees, then shouted again. "There's nothing else we can do now. Our truck is out this way. We'll meet you back at the road." They headed off in another direction out of the bush. Cosmos didn't even look at them.

"March!" he said, pointing us back where we'd come from.

"But, Mr. Greene, I—"

"Silence! March!"

When we got back out to the road, Cosmos told us to stand next to his car.

"Wait here."

We didn't dare speak.

And so we waited, for the longest time. It was hard to figure out what he was doing. He kept looking up the road. Finally, a truck came around the corner and headed towards us. We could see Barrett behind the wheel and Vander Zalm beside him. They slowed and Barrett leaned out the window to speak. But Cosmos ignored him and walked right past. What was he doing? Alice and I looked at each other in bewilderment. Soon an even bigger truck came around the corner. It was moving at a pretty good clip. When the driver saw Barrett's truck, he swerved to pass.

That was when Cosmos Greene stepped into the centre of the road. The truck was speeding towards him. And he stood as still as a statue, right in its path!

Alice screamed.

10

THE TRUTH

The truck came grinding to a halt, gravel flying everywhere. When it finally stopped, its licence plate was snug against Cosmos's knees. The driver leapt out of the truck and made for him, his face turning an interesting shade of purple.

Down the road ahead of us, Barrett and Vander Zalm stepped on the gas and tore off, clearing out. As they did, they passed another car coming towards us. It slowed and pulled over. What was going on here?

Out of the front doors of the car came Lance Bennett and Carol Lewis. Behind them four reporters who had been at the boardwalk shoehorned themselves out of the back seat. Bennett glanced back at Barrett's disappearing car a few times, looking a bit unsure, but soon fixed his eyes and a big smile on the scene in front of him.

This was getting even more confusing.

"Ah, there he is!" Lance shouted, eyeing Cosmos. He intercepted the purple-faced driver, handed him something, and sent him back towards his big truck. "Here's your expert!" he called out to the reporters. "Talk to him. Cosmos Greene is his name. I hear he was just out there, in the forest!"

As the reporters rushed towards Cosmos, Lance moved up close to him and whispered in his ear.

"Word leaked out. Small town, I guess. Thought I'd bring the media for you. It was perfect: they were still here! I'm wining and dining them for a few days. It's wonderful news! I know you've always hoped for this."

Then Lance looked our way, a little surprised to see us.

But Carol didn't even notice Alice.

"Mr. Greene, let me introduce you." She smiled. "This is Ms. Kim, *Vancouver Province*; Ms. Campbell, *Vancouver Sun*; Mr. David, *Kamloops Daily News*; and Mr. Foster, *Kelowna Daily Courier*." She turned to the reporters. "Why don't you ask your questions in that order?" She was really turning on the charm, like she had a switch she could flick or something.

"What did you see out there?" asked Kim in a demanding voice.

"Did you film it?" interrupted Campbell.

"Please," insisted Carol, "one at a time."

"None at a time!" shouted Cosmos. "I'm not answering questions!"

With that he turned back towards the big truck.

"Mr. Greene?" asked Lance, sounding a little nervous.

"Open the back of this truck!" Cosmos demanded, pointing a finger at it.

The back of the truck?

The driver didn't move. Cosmos turned to Lance. "Mr. Bennett?" he barked, as if it were Lance's vehicle.

"Why would *I* have anything to do with *that* truck?" Lance snapped, looking a little guilty.

"For the same reason that you brought these reporters out here."

"I don't understand."

"All right, have it your way."

Cosmos stomped over to the truck.

"Carol," hissed Lance between his teeth, "get the reporters back to the car. Now!"

She ushered them away. When one resisted, she gently pushed him, then smiled pleasantly. As she herded them back, she finally noticed her daughter. "Alice?" she said. "What are you doing here?"

But Alice ignored her as we moved towards the rear of the truck. What was it that Cosmos was after? What was inside? Cosmos reached down and pulled the big back door up. It snapped to the top with a clang.

"This isn't necessary" seethed Lance.

But he was too late. Sitting in the back of the truck were the two huge sumo wrestlers. One was wearing a purple kimono, the other scarlet red. They looked a little startled, though I had the feeling these guys were pretty hard to startle.

"I WANT TO KNOW," screamed Cosmos, looking a little crazy now, "HOW MUCH YOU GUYS WEIGH!"

Now they really did look startled. Or maybe just confused. They stared back at Cosmos, who seemed to have lost it.

"They're Japanese," said Lance, trying to regain his smoothness, "they don't speak much English. They were likely just visiting the park."

"In the back of a truck?" asked Alice.

Lance glowered at her.

"How much do they WEIGH?" repeated Cosmos.

Lance tried to smile. "Their names are Akekariya and Takanosakic, that's all I know. They were here doing publicity for Sony Pictures when I engaged them. They have a flight to catch to Tokyo. We should let them go." He tried to pull the door down again, but Cosmos grabbed his arm.

"I'd put their weight at eight or nine hundred pounds combined," he snarled.

Bennett looked uneasy.

"And they aren't slow, are they? They're lightning in the ring and many of the good ones can actually run like the wind. Isn't that right, Mr. Bennett?"

"I have no idea."

"Isn't their strength...legendary?"

"If you say so, Mr. Greene."

"In fact, I'd say one of these guys could easily CARRY THE OTHER ON HIS BACK...AND RUN AT TOP SPEED!"

There was dead silence.

Lance Bennett had been about to say something else, probably repeat that it was time for the wrestlers to go. But he had stopped with his mouth wide open. I looked over and saw an expression a bit like fear growing on his face.

Cosmos put a foot up on the back of the truck, raised himself into it, and walked towards the biggest sumo wrestler. Akekariya stood up, towering over the old man, looking as regal as a king. He bowed. Cosmos plucked something off his kimono and held it up. It was a pine needle.

"Been out in the forest, champ?"

Akekariya bowed again, a slight smile on his face.

Cosmos bowed back, then turned to us.

"The best way to simulate a sasquatch's footprints is to put on a hairy monster suit with a giant pair of shoes and…carry someone else on your back. That will press the footprints down into the earth and make, shall we say, a very deep impression. Eight or nine hundred pounds would do the job quite nicely. Don't you think, Mr. Bennett?"

"You have no proof that they did any such thing," said Lance, who was sounding like a real human being. There was nothing fake or smiley about him now. He looked like someone had just smashed his piggy bank.

"I'd say a sasquatch suit would fit these guys quite nicely," continued Cosmos. He eased himself back out of the truck, then motioned down the road in the direction that Barrett and Vander Zalm had fled. "And the acting talent in Vancouver is wonderful, isn't it?"

Cosmos paused for effect. Then he reached into the truck and pulled a blanket off something. It was a cage. Seven skunks were lying in it, looking fast asleep, drugged into a stupor.

Lance snatched the blanket from him, threw it back into the truck, and slammed down the door. "Drive!" he shouted, and the truck pulled away.

"You're going to have to get up much earlier in the morning to fool me, Mr. Bennett. The footprints were good, but not good enough. The odour is like rotting meat, not skunk spray. And your sasquatch? It didn't run anything like an ape."

Bennett shuffled his feet. "Why don't we keep this between ourselves," he suggested in a whisper. "A little publicity wouldn't hurt the town, you know. That's all I was after. It was harmless. Good for business. You want new businesses, don't you?" It almost sounded like a threat. But Cosmos wasn't buying it. So, Lance turned and scurried towards his car. The reporters had been kept there, far away from the action. I noticed one of them trying to open a door. Carol had locked them in.

But something still didn't make sense.

I rushed after Lance.

"Why'd you get them *both* to dress like sasquatches?" I asked him.

"Both?" responded Lance as he got behind the wheel

and slammed the door. "Only one wore a suit." He started making a U-turn.

One sasquatch? *So what had I seen in the trees? What made that huge footprint?* Its face was suddenly in my mind. And it scared me.

Alice had moved up beside me. When Lance pulled his U-turn, he circled around us and ended up right behind Cosmos's car. For a second he was blocked. He was within a few metres of us.

"*Alice,*" I said, "I saw another one."

"What?"

"In the woods. There was another one...*I know it.* And a footprint. *A giant one.*"

I glanced up and noticed that Lance Bennett's window was wide open. Our eyes met, then he backed up in a hurry and roared off down the road. Through the back windshield, I could see Carol quickly handing him his cellphone.

11

CONFESSION IN THE FOREST

Cosmos greene wasn't in any mood to believe me about what I'd seen in the woods. I needed to talk to Alice. Alone. So, I told Cosmos we'd take the first shuttle bus back to town, and he could go on ahead. He put up a bit of a fight at first, but soon he gave up.

As we watched him drive off, Alice turned to me.

"You *really* think you saw it, Dylan?" She was staring into my eyes.

I nodded.

"Then we have to find it! We have to. We *can't* miss this chance!" Her face was lit up.

I was really torn. My pulse was racing. I wanted to

do this...and I didn't. A big part of me wanted to go home and curl up in my bed.

"But we'd need an adult to come with us," I finally sputtered. "One who has what it takes to track it...who understands, who will listen to us. Seen any of those around lately?"

We looked at each other. We were both thinking the same thing.

Uncle Walter.

Then Alice sighed. "But he's retired...from everything."

At that moment I realized what I really wanted from my uncle. I wanted him to be what he once was. I wanted him to lead me on this amazing adventure.

"Let's un-retire him," I snapped.

"But we don't even know where he is."

"Oh yes we do."

"We do?"

"Think about it. Where do you think he'd go if he wanted to be alone?"

I could almost see the light bulb turn on above Alice's head.

We weren't far from the spot where Walter had driven into the trees with his Hummer while we'd hidden in the trunk. We were sure we could find it, and then all we had to do was follow the tracks through the bush.

But when we got to where he'd entered the forest, his vehicle wasn't anywhere to be seen. What did that mean? Worried, we kept going.

It must have taken us an hour to find the hideout.

By the time we arrived the sun was almost setting over Harrison Lake. The trees were waving gently in the darkening sky, like giants warning us. It took us a while to actually find the stump, even though we were standing right near it. I hadn't realized how perfectly it was camouflaged. We couldn't even see the tree fort, high above us.

We pulled up the stump and went underground. Not long after, we were climbing up the spiralling staircase and then stepping out onto the wooden floor. At first, we thought the place was empty. It was very dark. But at the far end of the room, in the shadows, we could make out a faint light, candlelight. And soon we could see Uncle Walter sitting there, just staring into space.

"Dylan?" he asked quietly, without even turning around.

"Yes?"

"Alice?"

"Yes, Mr. Middy."

"She fell off my back," he said out of the blue, very quietly.

I knew what he was going to tell us. We sat down at his feet.

"That's her picture that you saw in my hallway. I suppose I was old enough to know better...carrying her on my back across a high wire. She waved at the crowd, just waved, and then she slipped, fell more than a hundred metres. To her death. I didn't really do anything wrong: it was that wave that caused it. But you know, if you play with fire, you get burned. I haven't been on a high wire since that day. It's been more than ten years."

"Dad said something about it when he was mad at me, something about your dead wife."

"They hate me for many reasons. But that's the biggest. And they're right. She was a friend of the family. They think I lured her into the circus. But she wanted adventure. And I loved her. I really did."

He grabbed an oil lamp on a table beside him and turned it up. A glow filled the room. I could see a tear rolling down his cheek.

"A thrilling life? Thrills get you killed."

I knew it was time to tell him something I'd wanted him to know ever since we met.

"I got scared too, you know, very scared," I said, "last week." I swallowed hard. "Me and my friends got lost in a park in Alberta and some weirdo came after us. It freaked me out. *Really* freaked me out. More than I've told anyone." Alice looked into my eyes.

"At first, I didn't want to do anything. I just wanted to get away from everything. But you can't. Can you?"

"No," said Walter, "not from everything."

"I got so down that I wondered if I'd ever get back up. But these last few days, I've made up my mind not to be afraid any more. It started when I met you…you weren't what I thought you'd be."

Walter shifted uncomfortably in his chair and remained silent.

"There's danger in lots of things, Uncle Walter. But if you give up on adventure then you might as well be dead."

There was silence in the room.

"I'm for adventure," smiled Alice, "big time."

"We were out in the forest today…with Cosmos Greene," I said.

Uncle Walter looked surprised.

"There was a sasquatch sighting. But it was a hoax," explained Alice.

"But then…" I hesitated.

"Then what?" asked Walter.

"I thought I saw something."

"He *knows* he did," explained Alice. "And he saw a footprint too, one that was way bigger and wider than the fake ones."

"A bigger footprint?" asked Walter. He looked interested for a second, then dropped his voice again. "You were dreaming, Dylan. The sasquatch story is a folk tale. It's for children. And even if it were real, getting anywhere near it would be incredibly dangerous."

"Cosmos Greene says he thinks you've seen one," said Alice.

Walter shifted uncomfortably in his chair again.

"No," he murmured.

I stared at him until he looked up and met my eyes. "You told me once that you don't like to lie."

Walter sighed. "I came to Harrison Hot Springs to get away from things."

"But you knew about the legend," said Alice.

Walter didn't answer.

"We want to see it!" continued Alice. "Come with us!"

Walter stood up. "This time I walked, all the way. Left my Hummer at home. So I can't get you two home tonight like I should, not in the dark forest. Here's what's going to happen: I'm going to bed, and so are you two—there are some sleeping bags and pillows around here—and in the morning I'm taking you back to your parents."

HE DIDN'T SLEEP ANY BETTER than we did. In the middle of the night, he seemed to have a nightmare because he cried out. Not long after that, he got up and sat by a window, gazing into the starlit sky. I came over and sat beside him.

"I'm looking for Poe," he whispered, smiling slightly.

We sat in silence for a while.

"Lance Bennett was there today. He was the one who made up the hoax, for publicity I guess."

"I'm not surprised. In the circus, you learn to read a face, right through to the soul."

"After, he heard me telling Alice about the other one and the big footprint, and then he just tore off in his car talking on his cellphone."

Walter looked alarmed. He stood up and started to pace. "He did?"

"Yeah, so what?"

"Nothing."

He sat down again. An owl hooted somewhere in the darkness.

"You saw one, didn't you?" I whispered. "You saw a sasquatch."

I *really* wanted to know.

Alice crept out of her sleeping bag and crawled towards us. Walter wasn't saying anything.

"We're going after it," said Alice.

I had made up my mind too. I wanted to look this Reptile in the face.

"We're going, no matter what," I echoed. "And if we go alone, who knows what will happen to us? We need you, Uncle Walter, to keep us alive. You *have* to come."

He didn't answer. But I could see he was thinking.

THE NEXT MORNING WALTER had us up before the sun had even risen. He made us an amazing breakfast of pancakes with strawberries and whipped cream and maple syrup. I couldn't understand how he came up with it all.

When we finished we all sat silently at the table for a few minutes.

Walter knew that he couldn't force us to go back to our parents: couldn't carry two fourteen year olds all the way back to Harrison Hot Springs, kicking and screaming. We had made it clear that we were heading into the forest after the sasquatch. But did he believe we'd do it? Would he come with us, or would he take the chance that we'd turn back after a while? Would Mom and Dad want him to abandon us?

I wondered what he had decided. And what was in his heart anyway? Was the spirit of adventure, the spirit that seemed to have died with his wife, still alive somewhere deep inside him?

"I think Lance Bennett believes you saw a sasquatch," Walter said suddenly. "He must have seen the look in your eyes that I saw last night. His men made some pretty big footprints...and the one you saw was bigger. He knows you have no reason to lie."

He paused.

"You know that stretch of land he has along the beach where he's putting up his monster candy store and all the nonsense that goes with it?"

"Yes."

"Word is he has five times as much property as that, all along the boardwalk. You think Harrison Hot Springs is a sasquatch place *now*?"

"Imagine if he could get an image of one!" I exclaimed, putting two and two together. "Or a video?"

"He's thinking bigger than that," said Walter darkly. "A man like Bennett could build an empire here."

"What do you mean?"

"If you were him and you fell into some sort of

reasonable lead that this creature existed, here's what you might do: you might call some people, some expert people. Catching it is nearly impossible, so they hunt it for you, *kill* it, and drag it down out of the mountains. Then you have it stuffed and put on display near the beach—and you *own* this town, and half the tourism dollars in the best tourist province in Canada, the most beautiful place in North America. You would have solved one of the greatest mysteries in the world and have proof of it in flesh and blood…and the world would beat a path to your big, shiny door."

It made perfect sense. Just filming a sasquatch wouldn't be enough for a guy like Lance; maybe people wouldn't believe him, maybe it would get away….

"Bennett was likely calling people in Vancouver on his cell." Uncle Walter paused. "Someone has to stop them." His voice was rising.

This sounded promising.

"Do you think Dylan *really* saw one?" asked Alice. Walter shifted his eyes back and forth, looking at us. Slowly his face lit up with an energy I had never seen before. It must have been the sort of glow that came over him when he walked the high wire.

"Which direction was the footprint pointing? The sun would be in the west."

"Uh," I thought back, "uh, west then, I guess... northwest."

"If it's real, then I know where it's going," said Walter to himself. He smiled. "We could track it."

"We?" I asked. My heart leapt. *What was he saying?* "Well," said Uncle Walter, "I can't let you guys have all the fun."

Alice started jumping up and down like a kid. "Where's it going?" she cried.

"Towards Hell's Gate Canyon," replied Walter, his eyes narrowing, "where the water roars down the Fraser River like the devil has churned it, where Indigenous people and early European explorers lost their lives... where, long ago, *I saw a sasquatch.*"

A shiver went through me.

"It was about twenty years ago, in circus days... when I was a star. I used to travel all around the world. I'd look for things to exhibit. They were all fakes. But the sasquatch, that was different. I believed it was true. And I was desperate to find one. Then one night near Hell's Gate Canyon I came to a clearing in the woods and I saw something in the distance—big and black, hands like a giant's—with its back to me, eating leaves off a tree. It turned and saw me, and ran. I tried to convince myself that I was dreaming. *But I know what*

I saw. I kept trying to find the time to get back here. I couldn't. Then, when the accident happened, I stopped everything. After I retired, I moved here. I guess I just wanted to be close…to something amazing."

Walter stood up.

"I'm *not* letting you go alone," he announced. "I'm *not* missing this chance. And I'm not letting Lance Bennett kill anything!"

He reached behind his chair and grabbed two bulky items in each hand. He threw one at me and handed the other to Alice. He seemed to suddenly have incredible energy.

"You each need one of these," he barked. They were backpacks. He must have packed them after he got up. They felt really light, and yet you could tell there was a lot of stuff crammed into them. Moments later, after we climbed out of the hideout, he had a big pack on his own back. He also had an old video camera, much smaller and nicer than Cosmos's, slung over his shoulder and the binoculars around his neck, but as far as I could tell, not a single weapon, at least not visible. It was still very early. The sun, barely risen, was shining through the tops of the trees in thick rays.

"Uncle Walter," I stopped him. "What about Mom and Dad?"

In the flurry of excitement I had somehow pushed them out of my thoughts. But now, as the crunch came, they were speeding back in. I was burning with guilt. I had no way to contact them. Mom and Dad were old fashioned; I wasn't allowed to have my own cellphone yet. "Next year" they both promised. Alice didn't seem to have one either, which I thought was kind of weird.

"Thought of that, believe me," replied Walter, who was definitely not a cell sort of guy. "I'll send a note to them somehow…today."

"Good," I said.

Alice and I turned and looked into the wilderness. I wondered if I had the guts to do this. But Uncle Walter was standing bolt upright, his chest out.

He took a deep breath.

"Let's chase the dragon," he said, and started walking into the woods.

12

AFTER THE MONSTER

First we had to track our way back to the spot where I had glimpsed that figure in the woods. Walter led the way and set a pretty fast pace. It didn't seem to take any time at all. We moved swiftly along the forest floor, stepping over fallen logs, almost running in places, our feet crunching on the ground, and soon the fake sasquatch tracks appeared. Many of them had faded, but Walter barely looked at them anyway. He just kept moving forward like a bloodhound on a trail.

Alice and I knew we were at the right place the minute we arrived.

"Which way, Dylan?" asked my uncle. This was the

old Walter Middy, the one I'd only seen glimpses of. He was excited. He looked ready for anything.

"Uh…" I moved slightly, over to the same spot where I'd been when I looked through the binoculars and caught sight of that ghostly form. "Right…there."

I was pointing to an area about thirty metres away. The trees looked very dense. So dense, in fact, that I was a little worried: images seemed to poke out of the green darkness, as if a million eyes were looking our way, shadowy and leering. Had I imagined it? Walter led us directly to where that towering dark figure had been.

It didn't take him long to find the bigger track… then he found more. He looked at them and nodded his head. Soon he noticed something else.

"You see this?" he asked, sounding excited.

He was holding a small tree in his hand. It was about the width of a man's wrist. It was broken off about two metres from the ground, like it had been twisted.

"Everybody who has ever seriously searched for a sasquatch says they have a habit of grabbing trees and twisting them in their hands until they snap."

"Why would they do that?" I asked. It seemed like a strange habit.

"No one is sure. Some people think they do it when they're angry."

Gulp.

"Let's track this way," said Walter, motioning away from both the spot where I'd seen the figure and the twisted-off tree. He sounded pleased.

For an instant, I felt the Dylan Maples of last week coming back. What if we actually got close? What if it turned on us? What would an eight-foot, nine-hundred-pound animal that breaks trees with one hand do with my neck if I came into his territory? It seemed to me that if sasquatches really existed, then they must be desperately, *desperately* anxious to evade people. Maybe one reason no one had ever caught one was that anyone who had come really close had, uh, *disappeared* in the woods.

"Do you really think he's angry?"

"Who knows?"

I realized that I'd very quickly painted myself into a corner. It was like one of those dreams where you end up with no choices and everything is getting scarier by the second. I couldn't go back. And Uncle Walter sure wasn't going to stop now. We'd uncaged a lion. My only option was to plunge forward, help find whatever we were after, and then see if we could survive.

The forest looked pretty spooky. It was really damp where we were, with moss all over the ground and hanging from everything too. It was like a carpet, the greenest place I'd ever been, like someone had put a green tint over the world.

I kept seeing things in the forest. Bodies and faces darted here and there. Any second I expected something to scream and leap on us from the trees, or dart out from behind a huge stump. But nothing came our way. And Walter was finding more evidence. You could feel the excitement rising in his voice every time he spoke.

First there were other snapped-off trees, then more footprints, now heading westward towards the upper part of Harrison Lake. Whatever we were tracking was moving back in the general direction of the resort, but pointing slightly northward.

Now that I had the chance to look closely at these tracks, I could really tell that they were different from the footprints the sumo wrestlers had made. They were deep, with clear toe marks like Cosmos's casts, and so incredibly wide!

We started finding logs that looked as if they'd been tossed aside, pitched away in anger. And then we found a tuft of hair. It was on the bark of a big, dying Douglas fir right near a footprint. We all crouched down to look. Walter examined it for a moment, then passed it on, first to me and then to Alice. I felt a tingle when I held it between my thumb and forefinger. What if I were really holding sasquatch fur? It would be like having something in your hand that everyone said only existed in a story. It was dark brown and I could smell it without even bringing it near my nose. It had the odour of rotting meat.

"I've never seen this much evidence before," said Walter as we trudged forward.

Half an hour later we were still making a beeline for Harrison Lake.

"It's going straight back to the lake, just like I suspected. It's easier for him that way. There's a forest service road that goes up the east side of the shore. He probably walked it in the dark last night. Then he's heading north to Big Silver Creek. It's a river where they've spotted lots of sasquatch tracks in the past."

"So, that's where we'll find him?" I asked, hoping that we at least wouldn't have to go too far to meet our fate.

"No," said Uncle Walter. "From there, he'll turn and go northeast along Big Silver, then straight east across land and over the mountains. It's about thirty kilometres to Hell's Gate that way. That's where I saw the creature. That's where he seems to be going, somewhere near there."

He was talking really fast. It was obvious that his mind was racing.

"We have two options," he continued. "We can head to town, pick up my Hummer, drive over to the Trans-Canada Highway, and motor up the Fraser River Canyon to the tourist place at Hell's Gate. They have an air-tram there that brings visitors over the river at a really deadly spot: unbelievable rapids. It'll be fast, and we'll be close to where he comes out. We can go into the forest and see if we can meet him coming back from over here."

That sounded good to me: the three of us in a nice warm vehicle heading towards a tourist destination.

"Or," continued Walter, "we can hike our way out to the lake, westward, like he's doing. We'll be there in less than an hour. Then we can hitch a ride north from someone in a boat, get to Big Silver Creek, and then find our way eastward across land to the west side of Hell's Gate, following him. It's a longer route. We'll have to camp out somewhere in the mountains."

Door number one, please.

"I like it!" cried Alice. "That way we're going the same way he's going. That way we aren't near the tourists. He'll be trying to avoid them. If we drive, we'll lose the trail. If we go this route maybe we'll see him on the way!"

"I like it, too," continued Walter, kind of glancing at me to see my reaction. He looked away quickly. "It's fishing season. We should be able to find somebody who will get us up the lake in no time."

"This will be great, Dylan! Just like the explorers!" yelled Alice.

Didn't quite a few of the guys who went with the explorers die?

"Yeah, sure," I said, "uh, just like the explorers. Let's go. I'm game."

I found myself bringing up the rear the whole time we made our way to Harrison Lake. The forest started to get thinner as we got closer. Then we saw the entire lake from the side of the forested mountain, stretching north and south in a great, thin fjord. The town was so far to the south now that it was out of sight. But Walter was right: there were lots of boats on the lake below.

Way up in the blue sky I could see a black dot, circling, looking anxious to fly north. *Poe.*

The hike down the side of the little mountain went fast and soon we crossed the forest service road and were standing on a rough dock. Walter unzipped one of the many big side pockets of his green sasquatch-hunting pants. Out of it appeared a huge whistle. For the first time I noticed something else. Right beside the whistle, hanging down in a sheath tied tightly to his body and camouflaged green like his pants, was a huge knife. Really huge. A machete.

Walter blew his whistle. Five minutes later a boat was heading our way.

"Hey!" cried Walter, "I know this guy! He's one of the best guides in the whole area." He turned to me. "He'll find a way to get word to your parents too."

"Walter! Walter Middy, you old rascal!" shouted a middle-aged man from the boat as it approached. He had a big salt-and-pepper handlebar moustache and was nearly the size of a sasquatch himself. His face was really tanned. There were all kinds of fish lures pinned to his hat and he had a thick vest over his jean shirt. He pulled the boat up to the beach and jumped out, taking Walter's hand in his own big paw.

"Mackenzie! Mackenzie Cook, you old con man!"

At that moment Walter could have asked his friend to take us all southward, back to the safety of Harrison Hot Springs. But you could see in his eyes that his mind was made up. They were focused northward.

Cook, who ran a company called Cascade Adventures, was more than willing to take us up the lake. He and the tourists on board were all going north anyway, past Big Silver Creek to fish for salmon.

The tourists were three guys wearing glasses, a bit overweight, dressed in clothes that were meant to be perfect for the wild outdoors but looked brand spanking new. We thought these guys were pretty nice at first. Then they found out that I was from Ontario.

"Is that part of Canada?" one of them joked.

"Well, you're in God's country here, my boy," said another.

Then they discovered that I lived in Toronto.

"Toronto?" the fattest one said. "And you're still alive?"

What a doink, I thought.

They were even worse about the sasquatch. Uncle Walter had just brought it up. He didn't seem to be worried at all about telling Mack Cook. And I could see why. Mack listened very carefully. The expression on his face was serious. But just as he was about to open his mouth, one of the tourists interrupted.

"Sasquatch? You mean Bigfoot, don't you?"

"Bigfoot is what the Americans call it, sir," explained Mack, looking anxious to continue his discussion with Walter.

But by this time all three of the tourists were roaring with laughter.

"Are you sure you're over sixteen years old?" another

of them asked Walter. "Can't be in a boat without a life preserver at twelve, you know." They all guffawed again.

"That's a good one," said Mack, rolling his eyes in our direction.

Walter just smiled. "The Salish people believe there were sasquatches," he informed them.

"The Natives?"

"The people who were here before anyone thought of calling your beautiful area 'British Columbia.' The spirits of their people live in the mountains here and they don't like hearing anyone question the great ape's existence."

The three men looked at each other, as if they might burst into another laugh.

"More nonsense," one of them sneered.

"An old legend says that certain white men who go north on Harrison Lake, north to remove fish from the sacred waters, find themselves marked, unaccountably, with the sign of the sasquatch: a black X on their wrists."

The three men smirked again and looked away. Walter was a total nutcase to them.

"He who finds the mark on the inside of his left wrist, the sinister wrist of the two, will be dead at the hands of the sasquatch by noon the following day, killed in an encampment on the Lillooet River as he sleeps."

All three men looked right at Walter when he mentioned the Lillooet.

"Gentlemen, if you have the mark, you should know, and beware. Let me see your wrists."

With that, Walter took one tourist's left hand in his and turned it over: nothing. Then he tried another's: pink and clean. When he got to the third tourist, he seemed to grip him the hardest of all. Then he turned over his wrist. There was a big black X on the inside just below the meaty part of the thumb.

This was the same guy who'd been bugging me about where I lived. "Uh…uh," he stammered.

"Don't panic," said Walter. "In order to qualify as a sasquatch victim you must also have a certain name within yours. That name is Nomis."

The tourist laughed. "The name's Simon, smart guy."

Uncle Walter looked like he was going to faint. "What's wrong?" asked Simon.

"Spell your name backwards, my city friend."

"It's, uh, N-O-M…I…S."

After that, the guy was pretty quiet. He kept trying to make jokes and smart comments but couldn't really do it. He kept looking up into the forest-covered mountains and straight ahead of the boat towards their destination in the Lillooet River. Walter had known all along that Mack took his clients there when they were going this direction. And Alice and Mack and I wouldn't dream of telling this guy about Walter's circus background. He'd obviously put the mark of the X on many customers in his sideshow in his day. And even I'd seen what the poor guy's wife had written out on his socks. His pant legs had pulled up as he sat in the low seat at the back of the boat, and just below where his thick hairy legs, hairy like a sasquatch, showed, it read: Simon Gray, North Vancouver, BC.

Nomis: what a great Indigenous name. Probably meant "idiot."

Mack Cook had us to the mouth of Big Silver Creek in no time. His boat was one of those jet-powered things, souped up and sleek, available for the big bucks to city folks. The *Thompson* could really fly.

He let us off onto a dock at a logging camp. As we got out, Walter was explaining more about where we were going. Mack pulled a dirty old map out of one of about a million pockets in his vest. Then he unfolded the map, popped a pen out of another pocket, and began drawing on it. We all crowded around to watch. He drew an arrow to a place called Big Silver Creek, then made his arrow veer northeast along something he labelled Shovel Creek. Then he drew some rapids on the map and the words "Granite Falls." After that, his arrow left the waterway and went through an "unnamed valley" to a mountain, across which he wrote "1,600 metres." He drew a line over the mountain and the words "mountain pass." Finally his arrow came to "Scuzzy Creek." The creek led to "Green Ranch Road" and out to a bridge over the Fraser River to Boston Bar.

"Boston Bar is the closest town to Hell's Gate Canyon," Uncle Walter explained to us. "It's right near the Trans-Canada Highway."

When Mack was done drawing on what appeared to be his only map, my uncle just stood there studying it for a while.

"Got it?" Mack finally asked him.

"I think so," said Walter.

"Just walk up this logging road on the east side of the river for about a kilometre until you come to a path on the left-hand side. It goes into the bush and down to the river. We have a campground there where we take folks for wilderness fishing. Just off the path you'll see an ATV under a tarp. Here's the keys."

He slapped a set of keys into Walter's hand.

"Drive that baby up the road until it ends. Just leave it somewhere there. Nobody will steal it, believe me, unless it's the sasquatch." He smiled at Walter. "Then, just walk into the forest and head towards the mountains."

Walter seemed to gulp.

"You got a gun?"

Walter placed his hand on his machete. Mack raised his eyebrows and nodded.

"I need another favour," said Walter. "I need you to get a note to John and Laura Maples at the resort in Harrison Hot Springs. Dylan here will write it."

"Sure," said Mack, "just write it on the back of the map. I'll be back home tonight and I'll make sure someone at the resort writes it out for your folks. Don't worry, I know lots of people there."

I took the pen. I'd been thinking a lot about Mom and Dad while we were coming up the lake. They would be totally freaked. They didn't deserve this. I hesitated for a moment, then wrote:

Dear Mom and Dad,
The man who gives you this note will tell you what I'm doing. I know it sounds crazy. But don't worry. We're okay. This was MY idea. Not Uncle Walter's. I needed to do it, and I wanted to do it. I had to face it. I couldn't be afraid any more. I hope you understand.
    Love,
    Dylan

I handed it to Mack. He glanced at it, nodded, and winked at me. Moments later, he and Walter slapped each other on the back. "Good luck," said Mack. "You know I don't believe in the creature, Walter, but bring me back a tape and we'll crack open the beer and popcorn and have a look."

The three tourists were on the dock too, to stretch their legs. As they settled themselves back into the boat, we could hear Simon arguing with the others. He was trying to tell them that he doubted the fishing was all it was cracked up to be on the Lillooet River and that maybe they should turn around and spend this "beautiful day" back at the resort.

By the time Mack and the Three Stooges purred off we were already moving up the logging road. Soon we found the path to the camp and the ATV under the tarp. Through an opening in the trees I could see the edge of Big Silver Creek, some of the cabins on this side of it, and the skeleton of a fish near a campfire. It was gigantic: the biggest fish I'd ever seen. For a second, it actually spooked me. It was longer than me and almost as wide! It looked like a monster: offspring of Ogopogo or something.

"Sturgeon," said Walter, noticing my look.

They were the prize catches of the Harrison Lake

region, massive fish that sometimes took two or three men to lift.

Soon we were racing up the logging road, dust flying up in great clouds behind us. Walter was really motoring. He seemed to like speed. Eventually the road got bumpier and we bounced around like we were at the end of a bungee cord. Then it became a path and Walter slowed. When the path disappeared into the trees we parked the ATV and got out.

There was nothing but a dense rainforest in front of us and a barely visible trail behind. I could hear Big Silver Creek nearby and all sorts of creepy sounds coming out of the woods.

We were in the middle of nowhere.

13

IN THE MOUNTAINS

We entered a world unlike any I'd ever been in before. My heart was pounding and Alice's bright blue eyes were getting brighter. It was a true BC rainforest: a thick, wet jungle deep in the wilderness. Big Douglas firs, some nearly three metres across, stretched up to the sky, cedars by their sides; vines lined with maple leaves hung in spidery curves; giant ferns of yellow and green towered over our heads; and monster-high shrubs were everywhere. Walter had warned us about them. They had big green leaves and spikes on them that could pierce your skin if you touched them. Infection would set in quickly. They were called "devil's clubs."

Uncle Walter had his machete out and was hacking down limbs, not just to help us get by, but to mark our trail in case we got lost. When the travelling was quieter, he turned on his iPod at low volume. We could barely hear the first song, whispering in the forest winds: "Imagine" by John Lennon, about being "a dreamer."

We kept close to the green river on our left. It was like we were following a tunnel through the trees. This really was the point of no return. There was nothing civilized between where we were and Hell's Gate Canyon. I wondered how long it would take, and if I'd make it. Mom and Dad were going to kill me, if this trek didn't do it first. They had been so relieved when I was found in Alberta, unhurt by the Reptile. And they'd spent every minute since then worrying about my moods. Now, before they had fully recovered, I was doing this, giving them this nightmare. But I felt driven to do it. I could only hope that they understood what I'd said in my note.

We trudged forward, all of us working hard at hiking. The thick undergrowth made walking difficult. Every now and then Uncle Walter glanced up. That black speck was still in the sky above us. Poe was like a compass needle we could count on.

Evidence that the creature had been here was all around us. We discovered more footprints in sandy patches on the riverbank and more twisted-off trees. Then we stumbled upon a marmot, or more precisely, its head, feet, and tail, ripped from the torso and lying in a scattered trail, as if our prey had torn it apart while it kept walking. The blood was still clotting on the fur around the severed limbs and neck.

So far Uncle Walter was right. The creature appeared to be going where he thought it would go, taking the same route Mack suggested.

As we worked our way forward, the sound of the creek rushing along beside us and shapes moving behind every tree, my eyes were so wide open that it felt like I could see backwards. It made sense to me that a bear or a wolf or anything that could kill us would take advantage of our situation: three vulnerable human beings in their territory. And if there really was such a thing as a sasquatch, then what would he do? I tried not to think about it.

It took us a couple of hours to get to the spot where Shovel Creek meets Big Silver. But when we did, things got a bit better: the thick undergrowth got sparser, the trees farther apart, and everything was drier. Shovel wasn't very wide. In fact, it was so narrow that we almost went past it, thinking it might be just a little stream running gently over rocks. We turned northeast along its banks.

It was late afternoon when we started hearing something unusual. We had just entered a canyon, and sounds began echoing around us, rushing sounds that got louder as we moved closer. The creek, now pretty well a river and flowing much faster, made a sudden turn. When we came around the corner, we saw it. A waterfall: a big rocky waterfall right in the middle of the wilderness! I thought of Mack's map. Granite Falls: right on schedule.

It was awesome. It looked like some sort of monster mushroom, split in the middle with a wide island of stone and a stem of rock that dropped straight down, the water whipping around it and falling in two thundering cascades into a deep blue pool near us. Cool as it was, Granite Falls was a barrier. It took us half an hour to climb it, and when we were done our energy was nearly gone. I was starving too. I'd been so excited it hadn't even occurred to me what we were going to do for food.

Walter read my mind.

"Hungry?" he asked. Smiling, he set his big backpack down and began digging around in it, one arm thrust all the way up to the shoulder. Moments later he had produced a gourmet mountain picnic. It was amazing to think he had prepared it in the tree fort this morning. There was mixed mango-pomegranate-watermelon juice, red as blood and freshly squeezed, which he poured out of a big container into three elegant teacups; a salad of spinach, fresh vegetables, and sprouts with a tangy mustard dressing; and spicy Italian sausages that we ate inside buttered pita bread just nicely toasted. We cooked everything over an open fire, which he conjured up in no time. For dessert he made carrot cake materialize, with sweet white icing, and finally he boiled some tea, from some wild British Columbia herbs he'd found in the forest. We had a crazy tea party in the wilderness. It was all enough to make me finally relax a little.

But it didn't last long. Soon Uncle Walter had us back on our feet. From Granite Falls we had to strike out straight east into even more desolate wilderness: there wouldn't even be a river to guide us.

We had been going upwards since we left the ATV. Now everything opened up, the trees grew smaller, and we went into a valley. It was like entering a new room deep inside a labyrinth. Down we went and back up the other side. Then the ground started to get much steeper. A lake appeared, shimmering blue.

We began seeing more wild animals. Every one we saw seemed frightened of something. And it wasn't us. We saw a beaver beetling along near the lake and vanishing into it, smacking its tail with a loud crack; a mule deer running across our path, galloping at top speed. Suddenly we stopped in our tracks: a big black bear stood up and stared at us from a distance. We stared back. Then it turned and ambled quickly away, as if it had greater fears nearby. Somewhere, I thought, somewhere out there, whatever that creature is, it's moving at high speed, and everything in its path is clearing out.

Up ahead, we could see a mountain looming above us.

"Is that the one we have to cross?" asked Alice.

"That's the one," said Walter.

I remembered what it said on the map: 1,600 metres. It looked all of it. The sun was almost down and things were growing dimmer. The short trees in front of us looked like dark men, beckoning us as we approached; the lake water was a black skating rink and the open valley behind us a grey, stormy sea, blowing in the wind that was picking up. It was getting colder. Soon we wouldn't be able to see. Here we were in near-darkness, chasing a monster. We heard something howl not far away. My legs were dead tired. I couldn't go any farther. I just wanted to fall asleep in my warm bed back home, into a deep sleep where no demons lurked. But how could we sleep anywhere here? And we couldn't climb that mountain in the night.

Walter read my mind again.

"We're stopping here," he said.

He was pointing to a flat spot where a huge rock sat jutting up, a protective wall against the weather and everything else.

"Open up your backpacks."

Not only did thick sleeping bags come bouncing out, pillows sewn into them, but more food appeared, packed into plastic bags and Tupperware containers— soups, pastas, and all sorts of things.

Walter had his own sleeping bag in that magical big backpack of his and another package, green like everything else he seemed to use in the woods. He pulled it out, unsnapped it, freed up some pegs and strings, and started spreading out the rest. A tent: a big, glorious, green tent for three. I hated every last bit of camping equipment Mom and Dad owned, but Uncle Walter's stuff, on this dark night deep in the BC forest, was like a piece of heaven to me.

We didn't even bother with a fire. We put up the tent, laid out the sleeping bags, and crawled into them.

It seemed like only seconds later that I heard Walter snoring. Alice was quiet. I had the feeling she was listening, just like me, to all the frightening sounds in the night. But there was a smile on her face, barely evident in the darkness.

When I finally fell asleep, it felt like a deep one, like I tumbled downward into it and let it smother me. Down inside that sleep, I thought I heard footsteps, heavy ones coming up to our tent, pausing. There was loud breathing...then the footsteps moved away in giant strides. I struggled to wake up, but couldn't.

All I had was that weird sensation again, of looking up at blue sky moving overhead, then falling back to sleep.

IN THE MORNING EVERYTHING seemed calmer. Uncle Walter whipped out these little cereal packs, filled with granola and all sorts of healthy mixes, produced bowls and some milk, orange juice, and fruit. Before long we were off again, this time going sharply upward on the western face of our mountain.

"Mack thought there was a trail here somewhere," remarked Walter. Soon we found it.

About two-thirds of the way up the mountain the trees disappeared entirely. It was getting much colder, even though the sun was shining. Only our hard work kept us warm. The wind was blowing uphill, lifting us forward.

Partway up we heard rumbling.

"Get down!" yelled Walter.

We all crouched. It grew louder. The ground seemed to shake. After a few minutes it lessened. We stood up and looked cautiously out across the rocky landscape. In the distance a herd of mountain goats was thundering away, a mass of fear on the run.

It took us until well past noon, an hour after another of Walter's amazing meals, to get to our highest point on the mountain. We followed a winding path near the top and then headed downward again. The view was unbelievable. We were among blue alpine lakes and patches of snow, on land like the moon. Ahead of us we saw a sea of forest: no rivers, no trails, just trees. And nothing moved in those woods.

At first we went down through meadows, but then there were more trees and the forest got thicker and wetter. We were entering a rainforest again, one of those places that looked spooky and green with that thick, moss-filled carpet over everything. It made perfect sense that our creature would live here.

We were getting our directions from Poe, whom we kept glimpsing through the tops of the trees. But deep in this forest, it was becoming harder to see him. We followed as best we could, and walked until the sun began to set. We had to stop again. I was dreading it: this was going to be even creepier than the night before.

We found a spot that was reasonably dry, an opening with trees all around. There were leaves on the ground and we patted them down into a sort of nest, making things as comfortable as possible.

Before I went to bed, I stood and looked out at the land ahead of us again. It looked weird in the twilight, shades of darkness stretching out before us, black then dark, black then dark, like a ghostly chessboard. Our second day was ending. If the map was right, we'd get to where we were going tomorrow. Where on that dark chessboard would we find what we were looking for? And did I *really* want us to find it?

We snuggled into our sleeping bags. Hours passed and I lay wide awake. Uncle Walter and Alice had become quiet, so I figured they were asleep. It grew pitch black outside. I was thinking about Mom and Dad.

Suddenly, I heard those footsteps again! Then the heavy breathing. As the steps neared they slowed, as if whoever was on those feet was examining our tent. The nightmares I'd had as a kid came back to me in a rush.

Monsters chased me or came out from under my bed or slipped out of my closet and crept up to where I was lying. They would loom over me, their eyes glowing in the dark, their claws stretched out towards me.

I was frozen with fear in my sleeping bag. A shadow grew across the tent. It was huge. I could see the outline of a massive beast, standing on two feet, thick hair covering its outline. I smelled a sickening stench.

Cosmos had said that sasquatches are usually following you when you think you're following them.

It had tracked us. No one would find a trace of our bodies, and if they did, it would be like the remnants of that marmot: severed body parts, blood gathered where the bones were ripped from the skin.

I saw a hand reaching out for the door of the tent.

Then I saw another hand. It was Uncle Walter's, sliding down the outside of his sleeping bag. I glanced over. His eyes were wide open and his hand was slowly making its way to the sheath he'd left on the ground beside him, the one that carried his big, gleaming... machete.

14

FACE TO FACE

By the time the tent door was unzipped, ripped down by two humanlike hands, Uncle Walter was on his feet, the machete pulled back for a murderous slice, aiming just above his own head, neck-high on the creature before him.

"Hello?"

The creature could talk! It was also wearing a Vancouver Canucks cap. Uncle Walter lowered the machete.

"Everythin' okay here?" it asked, staring at the machete as it was withdrawn.

He was hairy all right, but he wasn't terribly big and he certainly wasn't a monster. He'd just loomed large in the shadow as he'd approached our tent.

"Don't get many folks in these parts," he said. "Thought I'd just check up and see if you was alive and well. My name's Adams: Lion Adams."

"Uh," stammered Walter, "where did you come from? I mean, it is the middle of the night...in the middle of nowhere in the mountains...."

"Right. Good question. Must seem a little strange. I guess I'm what other folks call a mountain man." He swept off his Canucks cap. "A hiker gave me this one day. I understand they're a hockey team?"

Everything else on Adams was made of animal skin or fur. His hair and his beard looked like fur too. And he smelled like an animal, one that needed a bath. But he definitely had the talking skills of a human being. He quickly made his way into the centre of the tent, sat down right in the middle of us and started to chat. In fact, we couldn't shut him up. I guess that's what comes of living in the forest. That, and the smell. Apparently he had a log cabin on this side of the mountain. Occasionally he trekked to Boston Bar for supplies, but for the most part he lived in the wilderness, hunting and fishing, making fish flies and clothes from animal skins that he sold to one of the tourist shops at Hell's Gate Canyon. He had come near our tent the night before but thought everything looked fine.

So why had he tried to break in tonight? It was hard to get a word in edgewise, but finally Walter succeeded.

"Why did you come back?"

Adams stopped suddenly. He looked like he didn't want to say.

"I thought you should know."

"Know what?" asked Alice, who was still sleepy.

"There's somethin' strange goin' on in these parts."

"Strange?"

"Well, the animals have been actin' funny since about noon yesterday. I have my own grizzly, you know, and one of those kermode bears that's white but born to black bears—Ghost, we call him—and seven bighorn sheep, and twelve mule deer, a cougar, and a mountain lion—they play together—and a pack of wolves. Two of the wolves can talk...well not exactly *talk*, but you know what I mean, and—"

"Adams!" exclaimed Walter.

"Yes?"

"What are you trying to tell us?"

The mountain man paused before he spoke.

"There's particular danger out there just now."

"What kind?"

"I don't know. I thought maybe you could tell me. It

isn't usual either, you know, for a man and two children to be walkin' around out here."

"We're not children," I said.

"Small fry, at least," he countered.

"We're after a sasquatch," said Alice in a matter-of-fact voice.

Adams looked at her, just stared right into her eyes. For a long time he didn't say anything.

"A sasquatch?"

"That's right."

"Just takin' a wild stab that there might be one in these parts?" he laughed nervously.

"No," said Uncle Walter, "we're tracking it. We've found footprints and torn trees. And they're leading us this way."

"Well...that's why then." He lowered his head, kneading the ball cap. "I *thought* I smelled somethin'."

It was hard to believe that he could smell anything other than himself.

"So, you believe in it? You think it could be around?" I asked, feeling breathless.

"Believe in it? I don't understand. Do you believe in me, young man? Ain't you seein' me, smellin' me, eyeballin' me?"

Smelling him, yes, for sure.

"So, you've seen a sasquatch?"

"No sir, for the most part, people don't see sasquatches."

"I did," said Uncle Walter.

Adams tried to stand up. His head hit the tent ceiling and he fell back down. He was staring at Walter now, his eyes wide. "There's a reason for that," he whispered.

"A reason?" asked Alice.

"Most times folks say they seen a sasquatch, it's a hoax. When it isn't...it either means you ain't right in the mind, sir, or the sasquatch has some reason for showin' himself to you."

"I think I saw one, too," I said.

This time Adams nearly ran out of the tent. He backed himself up against a wall so that he could see both Uncle Walter and me, as if he wanted to keep an eye on us at the same time. He looked back and forth.

"Never heard that before. Never met two people in the same room, two friends, who'd seen a sasquatch at different times. I don't like this. Somethin' is goin' to happen."

"Let's hope so," said Alice, smiling.

"Don't say that, child, don't say that."

"We plan to film him, see him up close," said Walter. "And we plan to stop the others from getting near him."

"Others?"

"We think someone from Harrison Hot Springs wants to kill it."

With that, Lion Adams let out a weird noise. He just put his head back and howled into the night like a wolf.

"Are you, uh, okay?" I asked.

"No. No, I'm not," stuttered Adams. "No one can videotape a sasquatch and no one—NO ONE—can kill it! It's meant to live in the shadows. It just wouldn't be right for folks to see it, to touch it, to see it lyin' dead somewhere, or stuffed. Somethin' would be wrong with the world. And there's enough wrong as it is. That's why I live where I live."

"But someone has already filmed it."

"That's a fake. If you get any real evidence, that will be the first. Footprints, pieces of hair, video, they all can be faked. But I'm tellin' you, don't do it. Don't do it! If you so much as see him again, just leave. In fact, you should leave now. Go home, I'm warnin' you. You don't know what you're gettin' yourselves into."

And with that he slipped out of the tent and was gone into the night. His whole appearance had seemed like a dream.

WHEN WE WOKE IN THE MORNING there wasn't any evidence that Lion Adams had been there. And none of us spoke about him. It was as if our mountain man never existed. He had been as nutty as an acorn anyway.

But we all seemed to feel what he had said. We started out on the last leg of our trek in a tense mood. We were about to cross into the rainforest where Walter saw his creature, and enter the Hell's Gate area. We had been preparing ourselves for this ever since we left.

It wasn't long before we came to Scuzzy Creek. It was perfectly named. It was a little waterway deep in the woods, winding around over stones and more green moss. Trees had fallen over it and strings of branches hung in the air like they'd been placed there by ghouls. Mosquitoes were out in packs, pursuing us through the woods. We could hear marmots, their frightened whistles echoing in the thick, damp air. We followed the waterway for a couple of hours, this time keeping it to our right.

We were desperate to find Green Ranch Road. It was the last piece in our trek and it would lead us out to the town of Boston Bar, the highway, and Hell's Gate Canyon. We knew there was an abandoned logging road beside Scuzzy that met Green Ranch, but had no idea where we would start seeing it. It didn't look like there'd been any logging done here in a long time. The trees were gigantic again.

Then, as we walked along, Walter said something that surprised us.

"I think I saw the creature right about here," he began, his voice sounding serious. "I can feel it. I doubt it's running now. This is its home. It's *here…somewhere.*"

He stopped and sat down. We gathered on a fallen log beside him.

"There's a place somewhere not far from here where the forest opens up and there's a swamp. I was going down a hill with the swamp in front of me. I leaned against a tree, I remember, to rest, and looked out across that swamp. *That was when I saw it.* It looked to be more than eight feet tall, and its shoulders were more than a metre across; the muscles in its back were unbelievable; its arms were hanging down to its knees; and it was covered from head to foot with dark brown hair. It kind of froze just when I did, like it sensed something. It turned, looked my way, black eyes glaring, and then vanished into the woods. The second it disappeared, I tried to convince myself I'd been hallucinating. But I know I saw it. I know it."

His voice was quiet now and his eyes were red.

"Did it scare you?" asked Alice.

"Yes. But not because I thought it would hurt me."

"Why then?" I asked.

"Because I'd seen it before...in my dreams."

At that moment I could have just passed off Uncle Walter as a nutbar. But I had a problem. I had seen a creature too, and the one he described looked *exactly* like it. That both excited and scared me. And the look that was coming into Uncle Walter's eyes right then didn't help things. He was kind of staring into the distance. Was he having a bad flashback? This was not the time to lose the only adult we had with us to a weirdo psycho brain seizure.

"Mr. Middy?" asked Alice.

But now Walter was standing and walking forward in a sort of trance. We got up and followed him. As he moved zombie-like through the woods towards something that his eyeballs seemed to be glued to, he started to talk again. He was using his quiet voice.

"Most people who know anything about the sasquatch claim they make nests in the forests. Sometimes they use caves or pile up rocks to make shelters, but usually they build lean-tos, with lots of trees they've torn down and lots of leaves on top...like...*right there*."

He was pointing straight ahead. My heart started to pound.

About twenty metres away, I could see a lean-to made of torn-off trees, mud, and leaves. It was camouflaged so you couldn't see it until you got close. And as we neared we started to smell something. Rotting meat. It quickly became overpowering, so strong that it made me want to throw up. I put my hand to my mouth and moved forward with Alice and Uncle Walter.

But he cautioned us to stand back. We didn't need convincing and stood as still as two statues while he kept inching forward. When he reached the nest, he peered slowly into the part that looked like a doorway, an opening about a metre and a half high. Walter moved his head so gently that it seemed he was afraid that just rotating his neck would make noise. His hand had slid down the side of his pant leg and found the handle of his machete. Now he was slowly raising it so that he could defend himself in an instant. Then he crouched...*and entered the nest!*

Everything was quiet for a moment. Then we heard a sound coming from behind us. We whirled around. It was like a shout, an inhuman cry; a deep shriek that pierced through all the other sounds in the forest. And in the trees, less than fifty metres away, we saw something move. It seemed to be coming right at us!

"Walter!" Alice and I screamed.

Uncle Walter was out the nest doorway in a flash, his machete held up, his face flushing red with excitement.

"IT'S COMING!" we shouted.

He pivoted and looked where we were pointing, then sped towards us. Keeping his eye on the rushing form in the forest, he slid in front of us like a protective shield. It made sense that we should turn and run, but I couldn't move my feet: they were rooted to the ground the way they've always been in nightmares when I've been chased. Alice and Walter seemed to have the same problem. We stood there waiting for the worst.

But immediately we could tell that the creature wasn't coming our way any more. Or maybe it hadn't even been running at us to begin with? It was moving away on an angle, crashing through the woods, faster than a big, speeding bullet.

For an instant we stayed put. We didn't know what this thing was anyway. Maybe it was another bear, or a mountain lion? We hadn't seen it clearly. Perhaps there were explanations for this so-called "nest," and even that smell? Maybe something had been killed nearby?

But in seconds all speculation died. A black laser shot out of the sky. It came at us as fast as it could go, past the tops of the trees and downward towards us, its target. Ten metres above us, it finally spread its big wings and swooped over our heads. Its feathers were ruffled, its beak open in a scream.

"Sassss-squash!" Poe shouted. "Sassss-squash!"

15

TOWARDS HELL'S GATE

That was when we started to run. After it! We sprinted straight into the forest, searching for the path the creature had taken, following those crashing sounds. It was either frightened or very angry because it was simply ripping things out of its way now: trees weren't just being twisted off at their trunks—some were actually being uprooted. It was shrieking and screaming, a huge beast on the run.

But before long the growls grew fainter. *It was moving at twice our speed!*

We looked up and found Poe, making frantic circles as he flew above the trees, constantly doubling back to find us, but moving ahead to keep track of the monster.

We could sense his fear. He wasn't merely after what Walter was after any more—he was terrified by the creature he saw below.

Keeping our eyes on Poe and on the trail being ripped through the forest in front of us, we moved forward as fast as we could go. Before long we came to the remnants of the old logging road, and ten minutes later we saw a clearing up ahead. Green Ranch Road! That road would help us tremendously. The creature wouldn't dare run along it in full view. It was more apt to just use it to navigate, sticking to the bush nearby, moving along beside the rough highway through the trees. But *we* could use it to make up time.

It was strange to be out of the woods. Our feet were freed from shackles. We ran along the gravel, faster than we'd gone for days. The road began to turn northward. It didn't take long before a sign appeared: BOSTON BAR, 5 KM. We were nearing the town!

But another half-kilometre along, we heard Poe shrieking. We looked up to see him flying east, away from the road, towards the nearing Fraser River.

We had no choice. We darted off our gravel path and into the bush. Sasquatch signs began appearing again. First the smell came back, then fifty metres into the trees we saw something that nearly made us sick. Lying across a twisted-off tree was a body of some sort, tossed aside. It was a large male mule deer, its neck badly broken, antlers crushed in anger, blood oozing from its nose and still twitching.

We moved on. In five minutes we could hear the Fraser, thundering through the trees. Then we reached a dead end. We had to put on the brakes before we all went flying out into thin air. We were standing at the edge of a rocky cliff. Several hundred metres below was the legendary brown river, the torrent of water that cuts southward through the centre of British Columbia like a massive ditch into the mountains, the route along which the Thompson people of the Salish Nation guided famous Simon Fraser more than two centuries ago. The explorer had hung on for dear life, fame and fortune in his mind, a rocky wonderland he had only dreamed existed appearing before his eyes.

The drop beneath us was breathtaking. It went straight down. Running north and south as far as we could see, a huge canyon was split in the earth. It would be impossible to get from where we were to the river.

The cliffs were just as daunting on the other side. We looked across and saw cars speeding by on the winding Trans-Canada Highway above them. We had come out of the mountains and the forest.

"LOOK!" shouted Alice. She was pointing at the river. Way down there, something seemed to be bobbing around in the rapids. It appeared to be dark. It was swimming!

"It's heading south, right towards Hell's Gate!" shouted Walter. "It knows we can't follow!"

It was a terrible feeling. I could sense Walter's frustration. I just knew what he felt. He wanted to jump. Just leap out into mid-air and hit those rocky rapids far below at terminal velocity, then ride the water downstream and find that creature from his mind, the one he had seen so long ago and wondered about ever since. But he couldn't. He'd be dead before he even touched the water. We were stuck.

Then things got worse.

Up on the Trans-Canada Highway across the canyon, a van pulled a sudden U-turn, swerving so abruptly that we could actually hear the tires squeal. Then it came to a jarring stop next to the railing on the shoulder of the road. Several men leapt out and rushed up to the canyon's edge, shouting and pointing.

"Binoculars!" demanded Uncle Walter.

I had them. But I didn't hand them over. I raised them to my eyes and looked across the canyon myself.

"Who are they?"

I brought everything into focus. There were four men. Three of them were wearing camouflage army fatigues and ball caps. Each of them had something in their hands. I focused again. Guns! High-powered rifles! And they were pointing them down at the river, following something through their telescopic lenses!

"NO!" I shouted.

But the men couldn't hear me.

"No...*what?*" demanded Uncle Walter. Both he and Alice reached for the binoculars. I pulled them away and panned over to the van. There was advertising on the side. I focused. TWEEDLEDUM AND TWEEDLEDEE it read. I whipped the binoculars back to the men and focused on the fourth one. There he was, shouting and issuing orders, the one and only....

"Lance Bennett!" I belted out.

"Lance Bennett? Where?"

"Right there, with his company van and three guys who look like snipers with high-powered rifles!"

"Oh, no," cried Alice.

"STOP!" Uncle Walter shouted as loudly as he could, but the men on the other side of the Fraser Canyon didn't hear a thing. "He must have found Mack's tourists! They must have told him we were going this way! We have to stop them! *They'll kill it!*"

As Walter shouted, a flurry of activity erupted near the van.

"What's happening?" asked Alice.

"They're..." I focused again. "They're leaving!"

Obviously, they couldn't get off an accurate shot. All four of them had turned and rushed back to the van. Lance took the wheel and the vehicle tore off down the highway, spraying gravel, heading south.

"That's good, isn't it?" I asked.

"No, it's NOT good. It's not good at all," exclaimed Walter. "They're following the creature. They're on a paved highway going 150 kilometres an hour and we're up here—on the side of a mountain, immobile!"

He had a point.

Alice had snatched the binoculars while I paused. She was training them up and down the river, desperately looking for a valley or a pathway—anything that might lead down to the river and give us some sort of access. Walter's eyes were darting around inside his head as if he was trying to make a decision about something, a very difficult one.

"Look!" cried Alice. She had spotted something upriver. "There's something in the water. Something big and yellow, floating this way—fast!" I looked down. There were several rows of people on board.

"That's it!" shouted Walter. "I'm doing it!" He seized his backpack and tore into it.

"Doing what?" I asked, worried what the answer would be.

"That's one of those tourist rafts they take people down the Fraser River on to make like they're a bunch of Simon Frasers."

"What does that have to do with us?"

"Not us, Dylan…me."

"What do you mean?"

By this time he had pulled a big rope out of the backpack and was tying an iron hook to it, so tightly I thought he was going to rip the rope in half.

"You and Alice are staying here! Make your way back up the road, cross over to Boston Bar, and sit tight! Find a restaurant and call your parents!"

He was shouting at me, even though we were only about a metre apart. His eyes were on fire, his face red, and I could see those old muscles—still hard despite the decade or so they hadn't been used on the flying trapeze and high wire—bulging under his shirtsleeves.

"What are you going to do?" asked Alice, swallowing hard.

Uncle Walter paused for a second. He looked at us.

"I'm going over the cliff."

Okay...he is going to commit suicide. Fine. Let's get our butts out of here and over to Boston Bar and into a restaurant and order some hot chocolate or soup. Let's phone the parental units and....

"*No*," said Alice to Walter as firmly as I'd ever heard her say anything.

No? What does that mean?

"If you're going, then we're going! Right, Dylan?"

I didn't say anything.

"I can't let you do that," replied Uncle Walter.

Good response, man.

"Yes you can," snapped Alice and she reached out and snatched his video camera from his backpack and dangled it over the edge of the cliff. "Let us go or I drop the camera. If it's gone...then why chase the sasquatch?"

Unfortunately, she had a point.

That's why, seconds later, we were all preparing to leap out over the rocky cliff of the Fraser Canyon together, and I was preparing to puke my guts out.

"Hurry!" shouted Alice, eyeing the yellow raft coming our way.

"Okay," said Uncle Walter, surprisingly calm. He seemed to be reverting to circus mode, to the days when he performed death-defying feats. Nervousness would be the end of you in that business. So, he was forcing himself to be as calm as ice.

"I've carried many people on my back before," he said aloud to himself, like he was trying to convince himself everything was going to be all right. "It was an accident."

What was he planning?

"Wrap yourselves onto me, grip me around the chest and the waist: Dylan on my right and Alice on my left. Hang on and don't do ANYTHING unless I tell you to. Got that? NOTHING! Just hang on."

He slammed the hook into a rock, digging it into a crevice. Then he tested it. It seemed secure. It had to be. Walter tied the other end of that very long rope (that had somehow been coiled up in his big backpack) around his waist. He reached into the pack again and drew out a pair of leather mitts with no fingers. As he put them on, I could see they were skintight. Then he walked to the edge of the cliff.

Alice moved with him.

But I didn't.

"I'm scared!" I shouted.

I couldn't move.

There was a long pause as they both stood at the edge of the canyon and looked back at me. Walter lowered his eyes, as if gazing into his past.

"So am I," he said.

An image of the Reptile flashed through my brain. I wanted to curl up on the ground.

Alice put a shaking hand on my shoulder.

Uncle Walter seemed to be sagging right in front of us. We saw the sadness spreading on his face. His shoulders began to fall.

I thought back over the past week. I thought of the progress I'd made and why I'd made it. I didn't want to be the shell that Walter had been when we first got here. I was glad I'd convinced him to have fun again. I didn't want to be afraid for the rest of my life. I didn't want to let the Reptile and all the monsters I'd dreamed up win. My parents could protect me from a lot of things, but not from my own fears. I *had* to do this. I had to face things. *Now.*

"Let's do it," I whispered.

Walter looked at me. We locked eyes. Then he straightened up. He stuck out his chin.

"Dylan: arms around my chest," he ordered. I wrapped my arms around his chest. "Alice: around my waist." She put her arms around his waist in a vise-like grip.

Alice and I were looking straight into each other's eyes. Our noses were almost touching as we rested our heads against Uncle Walter's chest. I could feel his muscles tensing.

"Ready?" he asked.

"Ready," said Alice.

We leapt out into thin air.

16

HELL'S GATE

At first it felt like we'd been shot out of a cannon—just fired into space. But what an incredible space! Beneath us the Fraser River and the sides of its rocky canyon were like some sort of gigantic IMAX film in 3-D. It was like a dream: one of those dreams where you're falling. I had this amazing feeling in the pit of my stomach. Alice's blue eyes, blue like Lake Louise, were right in front of me. And they were smiling at me. In my mind I heard one of the songs Walter had been playing a lot these last few days, about floating on a river with a girl with "kaleidoscope eyes."

"Hang on! Tight!" shouted Uncle Walter. I noticed

that he had the last ten metres of the rope bunched up in his hands.

A split second later he grabbed the rope. It jerked violently and he let go.

"Ahh!" he cried.

I saw it had cut through his gloves and scarlet red was oozing through the cracks. But he had slowed us down. In fact, for a minute we were just drifting in space. It felt like nothing at all. We hung in the air above the canyon.

"Again!"

The rope jerked once more as Uncle Walter seized it again and cried out. The blood dripped down onto his palms. We slowed a second time. And again we floated. It was an unbelievable feeling. I glanced up at the blue sky and watched it move by. Three more jerks of the rope, the last the most violent one, left us hanging at the end of our rope…so to speak.

But it wasn't over yet.

Instantly the rope began swinging us, very fast, right towards the canyon wall. Uncle Walter twisted as we moved, trying to slow us down. But the rocks were coming up fast.

"In the circus," shouted Walter, "if you can't get your butt up over your head, you're dead!"

I had no idea what he was talking about.

"Lift your legs! Use your stomach muscles! Lift your legs as high as you can and stretch them out towards the rocks. When we hit, let them give a bit. And push off! We have six legs here to cushion us!"

And so we slammed into the side of the Fraser Canyon at jet speed, our legs stretched out to take the blow. We all let them give a bit, like accordions being squeezed. It was jarring. My knees hit my mouth and split my lip. I looked over and saw that exactly the same thing had happened to Alice! But we were alive.

We bounced way out over the gorge again, came to a stop in the air, and then swung back towards the wall. The second time we hit we were going slower, and by the third contact Walter actually reached out and grabbed a rock, bringing us to a halt. We were dangling about twenty metres above the ground and the river. Directly below us was a ledge, a big ledge blasted out of the rock long ago. Along it ran a railway track, the tracks of the legendary CPR. They were five metres down. Bands of grass grew on either side of the rails.

"Drop!" instructed Uncle Walter, "*Just* let go and drop! Aim for the grass. And when you hit, do the give thing again with your legs. Then roll. Dylan first."

I dropped. I've heard that coming down in a parachute can be a pretty hard landing and this was probably like that. I kind of crashed into the ground and my legs smarted. But I was okay. I rolled out of the way. Alice came thudding down after me, and then Uncle Walter.

I wanted to rest for a while. It felt so good to be alive and on solid ground. But up Walter jumped. He swung around, raced across the tracks, and looked upriver. That yellow rubber raft was coming towards us, crashing through the waves, people screaming. It was hard to tell if they were happy or scared.

"We've got to stop them!" barked Walter. He darted across to the edge of the ledge, lowered his body over the lip, adjusted himself as he hung—and then did a flip, fifteen metres downward onto the narrow sandy shoreline of the Fraser River! He immediately got to his feet and started frantically waving at the raft. Though it was packed with people, no one seemed to notice. But then, for some reason, it steered its way towards him, banging around in the rapids.

In minutes it had hit the sand less than twenty metres from where he was standing and all the passengers started getting out, laughing and talking excitedly.

I could tell Uncle Walter was really surprised, though I could only see him from the back. His shoulders relaxed in relief, and then he turned to us and helped us down, getting Alice, and then me, to jump into his arms. I couldn't believe the strength the guy had.

Nor could I believe his energy. The second we were on the shore he ran towards the raft. The man in charge seemed shocked to see him.

"How the heck did you get down here?" he asked.

"Long story," replied Uncle Walter. "I need your raft."

"Come again?"

"We're after a sasquatch and I need your raft!"

"Run that by me *one* more time, partner."

"How much do you want for it for about a half-hour rental?"

"Listen, old-timer, I don't know what you're smokin' or how you materialized down here with these two children—"

"We aren't children," interrupted Alice.

"—but this here belongs to the Fraser Rapids Explorers Adventure Kompany, with a K. FREAK we call it: 'Get outdoors and FREAK out!' It's the best ride not in a carnival. A natural high! We, uh, don't rent this baby to anyone. You see those rapids down there?" He pointed downriver. "There's a spot there a few kilometres away called Hell's Gate. Believe me, it's well named. It's the narrowest spot on the Fraser, where the canyon just kind of squeezes the river into this foaming mass of water and rocks. It's as impassable now as when Simon Fraser and his guides avoided it two hundred years ago. If you go down there, you're dead. We always stop right here and portage past."

"Can't do that today, my friend," replied Walter.

"Eh?"

"I need that raft and I'm going to get it. I'm heading downstream."

"You don't say? Well, Mr. Wacko, read my lips: *we won't rent it to you*! You couldn't afford it anyway: it would cost you an arm and a leg, in addition to the ones you'd lose on your voyage."

Uncle Walter reached into his pocket.

"Here's my Visa gold card and here's the keys to my Hummer. If we don't make it, get yourself a new raft for the FREAK show."

The raft captain guy didn't look like he was into making any kind of a deal.

I could see Uncle Walter's eyes moving around, glancing over at the raft. The crew had left their paddles in it and he had noticed. Alice must have seen the same thing because suddenly she darted for the boat.

"Hey!" cried the captain, and made for her.

Walter moved like lightning, too. He stuck out his

foot, tripping the man, and then sprinted towards the raft. He leapt into it and seized Alice.

"Out. OUT! I can't bring you! I can't! It's *way* too dangerous!"

But Alice had driven her arm into one of the steel looped things that fastened the paddles to the raft. She was immovable. Walter looked up and saw the captain rising and coming towards him on the run, screaming. There was no time to waste. Walter climbed out, shoved the boat forward with a grunt, and sent it into the river. I stood on the shoreline with my mouth open. I couldn't believe that Alice and my uncle Walter were floating past me on the Fraser River heading straight towards Hell's Gate.

That was when I did something incredibly idiotic.

I jumped. I just leapt straight out into the air from the shore and landed in the raft as it went by. I have no idea why, but I did. Walter looked at me like I was a sasquatch. But he didn't look for long. He turned and faced the rapids. He had to take control of the life-and-death struggle ahead of us. We were about to shoot down the river at breakneck speed, like three skateboarders on a huge rubber skateboard facing a moving, raging half-pipe created by nature—the wickedest ride anyone could ever think up.

Lying in the back of the boat, hanging on for dear life, I raised my head and saw the captain and his tourists quickly getting smaller behind us, their mouths wide open, like a weird sort of choir.

"Alice! Dylan! Grab that paddle!" screamed Walter as we crashed into our first rapids and the front of the boat went almost straight up into the air. We stumbled and scrambled and fell over to one side of the raft and seized the paddle, using our combined strength to control it. Walter jumped over and snagged the other one. We all tried to sit up and face the front, paddles in hand, but it wasn't much use.

We were thrown around in the raft. The river had us at its mercy. Only luck would get us through this: incredible luck. Simon Fraser had big, sturdy birchbark canoes, a pack of hard-as-nails voyageurs, and a Shuswap chief when he came this way in 1808 looking for furs and adventure and the Pacific Ocean. He left his canoes north of here and just walked through the canyon like a mountain goat. He didn't dare try the river. The whole place just messed with his mind. I'd been reading about him in that BC guidebook. The land here was like a new planet to him, an awesome one. Above the river the grey rocky canyon went up in gigantic walls, then the mountains rose behind them, with huge green trees clinging to their feet and snow at their peaks. And we were seeing it all at a million kilometres an hour in raging water!

Alice and I were using the paddle to survive now—digging it into the side of the raft, bracing ourselves so we wouldn't go flying out. Water surged around us, slapping us back and forth and sideways. We'd rise up and then bang down. We'd be twisted so we were facing the canyon walls and then we'd go backwards. One second I was looking straight downriver, the next I'd see nothing but sky; then a huge rock would come at me, about to crush my skull, then disappear as fast as it appeared. We looked at everything through a film of water, white and brown. Adrenaline was surging through me as fast as the rapids shot through the canyon. We were soaked to the skin.

Walter was steering with all he had and screaming all sorts of things at us, but we couldn't hear anything clearly. The water was creating a wall of sound. It went on like this forever and soon I wanted to give up, just let the water drown me, suck me down, and smash me to smithereens against a rock.

But then I heard something Uncle Walter said. It was just two words, two words among the hundreds he was screaming:

"...Hell's Gate...."

I tried to find the river in front of us. For a second we lifted into the air and floated, suspended on a magic carpet in the sky, above the Fraser. And that was when I saw it: *the famous Hell's Gate*. The canyon was narrowing into a sort of tunnel, the walls rising up like the banks of a giant dam, and the river was a jet stream being forced through a funnel. I could see the highway snaking above us to our left. The tourist stop came into view beside it: parking spots, a sightseers' lookout, a ticket booth, and, stretching out across the gorge, a series of cables, like high wires. Hanging from those cables was the red air-tram, looking like a mini subway car. Through its windows people were standing up and pointing towards the water. They were about to start their journey over the canyon, across and downward, high above the river towards the half dozen stores and restaurants on the other side. To my right I glimpsed those stores, sitting on a big shelf near the bottom of the canyon about ten metres above the water. I could see tourists there, running towards the river, hanging out over the fences, pointing at something down-stream and at us slightly upstream. Some of them were screaming.

Directly in front of us I saw a bridge stretching above the water. It looked like one of those old suspension bridges I'd seen in historic photographs of Niagara Falls. It was red and looked awfully narrow. It must have been a footbridge. There were people on it and they were pointing too, upward, at something on the side of the canyon not far away.

We shot forward, approaching the bridge. But just as we neared the spot where the river was narrowest, the raft was pulled suddenly towards the ledge where the tourists were leaning out over the water. I could see them grimacing, others crying out, as we headed towards the rock-walled shore like a rocket. When we hit, it was what I'd imagined a head-on collision would be like. There was a jolt and we all went flying, really flying.

In seconds we were in the water, the raft behind us, sucked against the shoreline. The famous river had us now, white with rage. It ripped us forward. I went under and back up, and under again. I was gasping for air, seeing nothing at times, people looking down at me, horror on their faces. Then everything went calm. I could see blue sky and I seemed to be moving at a much smoother pace. I thought I heard my dad's voice saying something about the population of a town in the Alberta Rockies. I relaxed. Then, suddenly, I was back in the nightmare of the water, fighting to survive. I tried to turn myself in the rapids so I was facing downstream.

When I did, I could see that I was very close to the shoreline. The water was pushing us towards the base of the bridge and a wall of rock that jutted out. I braced myself to hit it. I did that "give thing" with my legs, like Uncle Walter had taught us, and smashed into the wall.

I felt a strong arm grasping my hand. I looked up and saw Walter, slightly out of the water. Gripped in his other hand was Alice Carr.

"Hold on!" he shouted, and with that he hauled us onto the rocks.

We both lay there for a few seconds, our chests heaving, as wet as seals. I could see people on the bridge staring down, pointing at us. A few started to applaud. Others were facing the opposite direction, watching whatever was up on the side of the canyon on the far side of the bridge.

"Up. Up! Let's move!" exclaimed Walter. I could see he still had the video camera strapped around him. In seconds we were crawling up the side of the embankment, making our way onto the bridge. It was wobbly up there and the pathway was packed—a dangerous number of tourists had raced onto it, drawn by the adventure unfolding around them.

As soon as we had a view, we looked up the side of the canyon.

Now I knew what people had been pointing at. Something was climbing straight up through the rocks. Every now and then we caught glimpses of it through the trees that somehow grew on the cliff. Then, for an instant, it emerged into an open space. I saw it as clear as day.

A sasquatch! A real live sasquatch!

There was no doubt this time. It was screaming as it climbed, and on its apelike face I could see something that looked like a smile. But it wasn't: not by a long shot. It was a grimace or a look of fear. *"Stay away from me!"* it seemed to say. But it had been caught. Hundreds of people were now looking at it in broad daylight. Nothing like this had ever happened before. The mystery of the monster of the mountains, a mystery that had lived for thousands of years, was being exploded. *The monster existed!*

We stood there, riveted.

Then there was a sound like shattering glass in the distance and another scream, right near us.

"Look!" cried a woman. "A gun! They're going to shoot it!" She was pointing up towards the air-tram.

We pivoted and looked. Way above the canyon, Lance Bennett and his three snipers were forcing their way onto the tourist car. One of them smashed a window and stuck a gun out, pointing it directly at the sasquatch. The air-tram began to move across the cable, downward, getting closer and closer to the other side, gaining a better shot for the sniper with every metre it moved.

"NO! You can't KILL it!" cried Uncle Walter and he started to run. In a flash he was at the gate near the end of the bridge where the air-tram would dock. And a second later he had grabbed the main cable and flipped himself up onto it. I remembered him telling me once that it was much easier to walk up a high wire than down one, since you can lean forward and press your weight into it. The cable went upward on a sharp climb from the floor of the canyon to the lookout and highway.

As I stood there watching, my mouth wide open, it dawned on me what he was about to do. The Magnificent Middy had returned! Uncle Walter was about to walk up that air-tram cable in the high-wire performance of his life.

17

DEATH OF A DREAM

Walter made his way carefully up the wire, leaning into it, his arms moving expertly in the air above his head for balance. Every now and then he would take one leg off his narrow path and stand on one foot, using his free leg to help counterbalance. His eyes were glued to the wire about five metres in front of him; his concentration on his art perfect. I imagined what it must have been like to see him when he was young, thousands cheering. I thought of what he had told me about running away from home as a kid: he couldn't stand to let his dreams die. "I wanted to fly," he had told me. "When you stand at the edge of a high wire, your mind tells you it's impossible, then…out you go."

I thought of something else he said, just the night before: "I believe there is a sasquatch, Dylan. I've always believed in things like that. I don't want to put him on display or humiliate him or anything like that any more. I just want to prove to myself that he lives, see him up close, and then leave him alone."

One of Lance Bennett's snipers had the gun trained on his target now. He held the barrel still. The air-tram was close enough that I could see his finger on the trigger. He started to squeeze it.

"NO!" shouted Uncle Walter as he jumped straight into the air off the cable. My uncle was about to show his incredible skill. He came down as hard as he could and the wire quivered like a snake crawling through the sky. It shook just as the trigger was squeezed. I could see the gun barrel jerk up. The sniper swore and swung around to stare at Walter. For an instant I wondered if he might train the gun on him. Instead, he turned back to the canyon wall and locked onto his target a second time. Again Walter jumped just before the shot was squeezed off. Again the gun jerked up.

The sniper glared at Uncle Walter. Lance leaned out the window and started cursing him. This was definitely the real Lance Bennett. There wasn't anything false about him now. He sounded exactly like himself. There wasn't even a trace of that smile I had seen pasted on his face so many times before.

The air-tram was getting closer and closer to Walter. But it didn't concern him. In fact, he kept, moving at a crisp pace towards it, his eyes concentrating on the wire, his arms in the air. I closed my eyes. I didn't want to see it slam into him. I could feel the crowd cringing. My heart sank. This was going to be his last show— he'd had one adventure too many. And I'd convinced him to do it.

Then I heard applause. I opened my eyes to see Uncle Walter on top of the air-tram! Somehow he had jumped from the wire and hit his mark. The crowd was roaring. Every time a sniper stuck a gun barrel out the window, Uncle Walter reached down and seized it in one of his strongman grips.

Three minutes later the air-tram had reached the dock and the creature was ascending out of view. They didn't have a shot any more. Walter lowered himself off the tram, dropped onto the dock, and raced up towards the bridge.

"Come on!" he shouted, waving us forward. Alice and I didn't hesitate, and soon the three of us were running between the nearby buildings, heading towards the base of the canyon wall the creature had scaled. We found a path winding up it, likely worn in by tourists, adventurers, and store employees. Our prey obviously wasn't a fan of tourist traps, and didn't know this one. The path seemed to rise almost all the way to the top of the cliff. We raced up as fast as we could, the creature high above us.

Then we heard shouts. Turning around, we saw Bennett and his thugs about a hundred metres behind, guns strapped to their shoulders. I wished these clowns would just give up! But they were coming on the run. Up we all went, moving twice as fast as we should have on this rocky path. In places it almost vanished and we had to leap from one ledge to another.

"Don't look down!" Uncle Walter shouted, in aerialist mode.

But I did. *Mistake!* I stumbled and almost fell to the floor of the canyon. From then on I kept my head straight up and my concentration turned fully on. Uncle Walter had once told us that he had a motto in the circus: "Pay attention!" He said it worked in life, too.

Beside me, grunting with effort, Alice seemed as determined as ever. Her eyes were turned upward, locked on the edge of the canyon.

Every now and then we glimpsed the creature. He'd glance down at us, with that look of fear or anger like a bizarre smile on his face. He screamed a couple of times. *"Leave me alone!"* he seemed to cry out. But we couldn't. We wanted to see him up close, look into those mysterious eyes...and save him.

Just before we reached the end of our path, he vanished over the upper edge of the canyon wall. Maybe he was gone for good. It must have taken us nearly five more minutes to reach the top. The path had disappeared and things were very treacherous. It was extreme rock climbing. We gripped ledges and edges and slowly moved up those last ten metres, terrified to look down at Hell's Gate below and all those people who were probably still staring up.

But we made it. For a second we dropped to our knees and just gasped for breath. Then we heard sounds that made us move: Lance and his snipers gasping for breath, right below us! We jumped to our feet and looked around for sasquatch signs. We didn't have to look far. There were tracks and twisted-off branches and knocked-over trees on a path that headed straight into the forest, making a beeline back in the direction of his big nest. He was seeking shelter, desperate to get away.

Seconds after we darted into the trees on his trail, we heard Lance and the others climbing onto the top of the canyon wall. Then the race was on. We all tore through the woods, our lungs burning, not knowing when the creature might suddenly leap out and grab us and twist off our heads like he'd done to the mule deer.

But all the signs suddenly vanished. There was silence in the rainforest. We stopped running and stood still. I looked back and saw Lance and his snipers doing the same. Their upright figures and the outlines of their guns were about fifty metres away, partially camouflaged by the big dark trees going straight up like bars in a huge jail. We all stayed still for a long time.

Then we heard a rhythmic thudding, like someone pounding something against a tree. It echoed in the forest.

"Indigenous people say sasquatches made that sound," whispered Uncle Walter, "thousands of years ago."

Alice shifted nervously from one foot to another. "What does it mean?" she asked quietly, as if she didn't want to wake anyone.

"I don't know. But people fled when they heard it."

Gulp.

Even those idiot snipers knew something was up. They had formed a circle and were slowly turning around, their backs to each other, looking out into the trees, guns ready, listening. Their circle was steadily moving towards us. I was looking the other way, but I could hear their footsteps softly crunching on the ground and Walter's and Alice's quiet voices drifting through the forest.

Then the steady, thudding beat stopped. So did everything else. It was so quiet we could hear ourselves breathing. The wind picked up, whistling through the trees. Poe appeared out of nowhere, the flapping of his wings sounding like a helicopter coming in for a landing. He swooped down onto Uncle Walter's shoulder. Then he pivoted, looked in the opposite direction, and gave a little gasp: a raven gasp. I will never forget that sound.

"Ahhhh," he said quietly.

Walter began to turn, then Alice turned too. He didn't shout and she didn't scream, but I could feel their horror, like it was something so real it was hanging in the air.

I slowly rotated my head.

Poe flew straight up into the air.

Standing in the woods about ten metres away was a nine-foot *sasquatch!* It was looking right at us. Half ape, half human, its hair was long and dark brown, its skull wide at the back with a ridge bulging along the top, its small eyes black and wild. It had a big, flat nose on a hairless face, huge arms hanging down past its knees—and that smile.

But I knew now for sure that it wasn't smiling. It was snarling...at us. It had teeth like a massive dog, and was rocking back and forth on its big feet.

This was the monster from my dreams. I was facing it. For an instant I hallucinated. I must have been dizzy, or perhaps my eyes rolled up in my head, because I had that weird sensation of blue sky again, passing in front of me, like I was moving along underneath it.

Walter had done many amazing things throughout the last few days. He had made a whole series of fantastic decisions. But he was about to make a bad one: a very bad one. He reached for his video camera and pointed it directly at the sasquatch.

It wasn't how his towering subject reacted that made this such a bad move. It was what it told Bennett and his snipers. They were still a good twenty metres away. They couldn't see what we were looking at, but when Walter went for his camera, they knew. They started to run towards us.

"Take the shot!" Bennett screamed, the adrenaline pumping through him and turning his face red. A vision of the legendary sasquatch monster stuffed and mounted in front of one of his many businesses on gorgeous Harrison Lake must have been racing through his overheated brain. He searched for the outline of the creature in the trees, his eyes bulging as if they would come out of his head.

He found it.

In fact, all eight eyes locked on the sasquatch as the four men screeched to a halt within ten metres of where we stood. Guns were levelled.

Unlike Uncle Walter, many of my moves over the last few days had been ridiculous, and at that moment I made one that topped them all. I bolted from my position and placed myself between the sasquatch and the snipers.

"DYLAN!" cried Walter.

"Don't!" pleaded Alice.

"Move," growled Lance Bennett, a snarl on his face worse than the sasquatch's.

It was strange: the creature wasn't trying to get away. It was still rocking back and forth, watching us. We knew that it could easily outrun us, that it could crush us if it wanted to. But it was as if it had given up. *You want me? Here I am. Do whatever it is you human beings do. Kill me, or leave me alone.*

It was a standoff...at least for a few seconds.

"Shoot over the kid! Take a headshot!" screamed Lance.

One of the snipers squeezed off a shot. It felt like I could see the bullet coming at me. Everything around it moved in slow motion as it exploded out of the gun and rocketed forward, turning in the air as it whistled past. It whizzed over me and I thought I could feel it cut through my hair, which must have been standing about a kilometre straight up towards the canopy of trees above us. It hit something behind me and the sasquatch screamed.

*Then…*he picked me up.

He just loped towards me and lifted me off my feet with a single sweep of one of his huge arms. I might as well have been a feather. The stench was overpowering. Now my head was almost directly in front of his, and the rest of my body covered his heart and his stomach— in other words, all the best parts to shoot. Out of the corner of my eye I could see something red trickling down from his upper body. But I couldn't look back— his gigantic arm had me in a vise-like grip, wrapped across my chest.

The sasquatch moved directly at the snipers. They had lowered their guns and their mouths were opening so wide it looked like they were fire-eaters, ready to swallow. We took three or four huge strides and loomed over them. The creature's breathing was loud. His big muscles flexed and his heart pounded so hard I could feel it. He dropped me with a thud, almost throwing me at the snipers. I rolled over and looked up in time to see him smack two heads together. The men staggered forward, dropped their guns and fell face down on the ground. Then he seized Lance Bennett and the other guy.

"Please don't hurt me! I didn't—" screamed Bennett, as sincere as he'd ever been. But just as his next word was about to sound, his head connected with the other sniper's with terrific force. His body was suddenly a wet noodle. He wiggled and wriggled, bent and swayed, then fell flat on his back. The sasquatch had done them all in like cartoons.

Then it fled, back in the direction we had come from.

Walter and Alice were still standing where they'd been when they turned and saw the sasquatch. "I'm *into weird*," Alice liked to say. Well, now we had weird all right.

I noticed that Walter's video camera was still in his hands and that its red light, the one that tells you it's running, hadn't been switched on. So did he.

"Oh, man!" he cried, looking down at it. "We've *got* to film him, even from a distance!" We leapt over the four woozy bodies and ran.

We quickly realized we'd been going in circles since we left the edge of the canyon, drawn around and around by the sasquatch. Within a minute or two we were back out near the top of the cliff, around a bend from where we had come up. On the other side of that bend and far below we could see the crowd of people, like toys, still gathered. Media vans were parked near the lookout. Lance had obviously alerted a horde of them.

Then we noticed something else. Standing at the very edge of the cliff, looking down at the throng who didn't know he was there, was the sasquatch. We had a clear view of him. He had his back to us. He looked as wide across as a couple of refrigerators. There was blood on his shoulder.

Cosmos Greene had told us stories about other sasquatches being shot by people: stories that no one believed, stories that ended with the sasquatch getting away. It was said that they could take a lot of bullets without going down. It was like trying to shoot an elephant.

We slowed to a walk and moved cautiously towards the creature. We got closer and closer. Walter pulled the video camera off his back and trained it on his subject. He flicked the switch on. Instantly we were recording a sasquatch, as clear as day, as the sun began to set over the Fraser River Canyon. The creature turned. He gazed at us with a longing look as we steadily stepped towards him. That smile of fear was gone. We came within five metres as he stared right into the camera.

I couldn't take my eyes off him. He looked like something someone had made up: an awesome character from a book, a creature from another world. He didn't frighten me any more. He just *amazed* me.

There were sounds in the distance, near the edge of the cliff where we had come up from the top of the path. As the sasquatch turned to them, we slowly made out the forms of several reporters, pulling themselves up onto the rocky ground, swearing out loud, not looking up. They were dirty and exhausted, but held on to their cameras and notepads and cellphones like they were gold. They hadn't seen us yet. They were nearly a hundred metres away.

The sasquatch looked at them, that eerie smile growing once more on his face. Then he glanced back at us, the fear increasing. He was caught. If he ran one way, he'd head right towards the reporters; if he ran the other, he'd come at us. Behind him was the sheer drop of the Fraser Canyon. I suppose he could have made a desperate charge and just trampled us. But it seemed as if he'd had enough of people. "You will *never* catch me," said his black eyes.

So he turned…and leapt out into the sky above the Fraser Canyon.

We rushed to the edge and looked over. He floated like a skydiver, his hands and giant feet stretched out. We could hear him scream. It was a deep shriek, like a giant crying out, and it echoed and then faded as he fell, a haunting sound swallowed up by the canyon. Three-quarters of the way down, he hit the big trees. We saw him grab at one treetop: it snapped off in his massive hands. That slowed him, and when he hit a second tree he held on. We watched, spellbound, as he shinnied down its trunk and then disappeared into the trees and away from us all, down the canyon towards freedom.

We just stared.

"Dragons live," whispered Alice.

I was stunned.

"You filmed him," I told Walter. "He's in your camera."

We stepped back from the edge.

"HEY!" shouted a reporter, spotting us. "It's that Middy guy and the kids." They began running towards us.

"Where's the monster? This is front page!"

Uncle Walter looked at me. "Yeah," he said quietly, "I've caged him. In two days they'll have the army out here looking for him."

He paused, eyeing the reporters coming at us, their faces excited, drool almost dripping from their mouths. Then he turned his back to them and looked out across the canyon. In the distance we could see the sasquatch's head in the water. He seemed to turn and look up at us for a second. Then he went around a corner and vanished from view.

"Free!" cried Poe, high above.

At that moment Uncle Walter made a big decision. He secretively slipped the video camera behind his back, away from the reporters' view. Then...*he dropped it over the edge of the canyon.* It hit the rocks far below and shattered into a thousand pieces.

"Mr. Middy?" cried Campbell of the *Vancouver Sun*, puffing up to his side. "Tell us everything! This is incredible, isn't it?"

"Tell you what?" said Walter with a very calm smile.

"About the sasquatch."

"What sasquatch?"

Campbell gave him a puzzled look.

"The one you chased up here: there are hundreds of eyewitnesses."

"Have you spoken to them yet?"

"No, not yet. We will."

"And how close were they to this...sasquatch?"

"Well, maybe three, four hundred metres "

"I think you'll find that none of them are completely sure of what they saw."

"But—"

"It was a bear. An unusually large grizzly bear. A male."

"But—"

Alice stepped forward. "It was a giant bear." She smiled at Walter.

"Yeah," I added, "a great big bear."

"I have been interested in the sasquatch for many years," continued Walter, "and believe me, I'd know one if I saw one. As you are aware, many people claim to have seen them in the past, even crowds all at once. But no reasonable, grown-up human being has ever believed them. Only children. You have to have hard evidence."

The reporters were all gathered around us now. You could see them sagging as they listened to our story. But then one of them noticed something over my shoulder. His eyes lit up.

Lance Bennett was making his way out of the bush towards us, staggering, feeling his head. One of the snipers was behind him, looking equally buzzed.

The reporters rushed towards them.

"Mr. Bennett, tell us what you saw!"

"I'll tell you all right," he growled. But before he could go on, Uncle Walter interrupted.

"Come, come, ladies and gentlemen, Mr. Bennett is the esteemed proprietor of one of British Columbia's most successful business ventures. Do you really think he could mistake a grizzly bear for a sasquatch?"

"Eh? A grizzly bear?" Lance sounded confused.

"Mr. Bennett isn't the sort to go around seeing sasquatches, especially without any evidence."

Lance looked around. It was dawning on him that the sasquatch had escaped.

"He's a grown man," continued Uncle Walter smiling, "a respected individual. He has a reputation to protect."

Lance was eyeing us, calculating.

"You may even find footprints around here," continued Walter. "They always have a way of turning up in the wake of these sensational stories. But as we all know, footprints can always be explained. They have been many times. Right, Mr. Bennett?"

Lance paused. Then that fake smile spread across his face.

"Yes, Mr. Middy, quite right," his smile not nearly as perfect as before.

"What happened to your head?" asked one reporter.
"Uh…bumped into a tree."

HALF AN HOUR LATER we had all made our way back down to the tourist area. All the snipers were on their feet again, walking on wobbly legs, all but Lance talking total gibberish. Not only were they telling tales of seeing a sasquatch, but of all sorts of other weird things they'd encountered in the forest: talking animals, children that grew and shrunk—you could almost see little birdies flying around their poor heads. Most of the crowd had dispersed and those who remained were talking animatedly. Some were saying they knew they'd seen a sasquatch, others claimed it had to have been a bear, or a man dressed up in a suit.

Walter did make a few statements to the press. He said we had indeed thought we were after a mysterious creature and that was why we had come through Hell's Gate Canyon on the raft. But we knew better now, he said.

"Everyone can be deluded at least once, I suppose. Every year, hundreds of people think they see monsters—the sasquatch here, the abominable snowman in the Himalayas, Ogopogo in Okanagan Lake—but really, they only exist in our imaginations… that's something of which I'm becoming convinced."

I could see my parents coming over in the air-tram before they spotted me. Mom was staring out the window, searching the crowd and looking anxious. Dad looked worried, too. If they'd been angry about what I'd done, their anger was long gone by now.

Then Mom caught sight of me. A huge smile came over her face and she waved so hard I thought her hand might snap off. I readied myself for her whole supply of hugs.

Once they got out of the air-tram they made a beeline towards me. I could see Mom was clutching something in her hand: a copy of the note I had sent with Mack Cook. I looked at Alice standing beside me, obviously feeling very alone. Her head was down and she was kicking gravel back and forth between her feet. Carol was far away in the crowd, with Lance, giving all her attention to him. I reached out and held Alice by the hand. I'd never done anything like that before. She looked at me. Then I felt her squeeze.

Uncle Walter was smiling at us. He came over and brought his face up close to ours. We were like a little island among all the grown-ups and their big opinions.

"We know," he said quietly, gazing deeply into our eyes, *"and that's enough."* He looked like someone who knew a wonderful secret. He seemed very happy.

Then he stood up and spoke in a louder voice as my parents neared. Mom was getting teary, holding her arms out to me; Dad was hanging back a little. Walter sounded different now. His voice actually seemed a bit like mine. I looked up at him and noticed for the first time how much he resembled me, aged, with a dashing goatee and moustache, built like an athlete still, and an amazing, dreamlike life behind him.

"The only thing I can't figure out," he said, "is how that sasquatch could look exactly like the one I've been seeing in my dreams since I was a child."

When he said that, I saw nothing but that blue sky passing above me again, looking peaceful like on a beautiful Alberta day. I wasn't afraid anymore, of anything.

I opened my eyes.

18

BACK INTO THE LOWER WORLD

Jefferson airplane was playing on the Jeep's radio. It was "Somebody to Love." I realized I had heard "White Rabbit," too, along with John Lennon's "Imagine," and a bunch of Beatles songs. Mom and Dad had found a sixties radio station.

Blue sky was passing over me as I lay in the back seat.

I slowly sat up. I must have been lying with my head facing the window and sky. I could see the mountains approaching as I wiped the sleep from my eyes.

"We'll be in Banff in twenty minutes," Dad was saying. "Banff has a population of 8,666 granola-loving souls."

What was going on?

I glanced around me. My earphones were on the seat, my BC guidebook was open at a page that showed an enormous rainforest. THE SASQUATCH read a headline on the next page, with a drawing and some casts of footprints being held by a rather hairy-looking older man. The model Hummer I'd bought in Calgary was on the floor. One of Mom's magazines lay beside the guidebook, opened at an advertisement for a natural-smelling perfume called "Unicorn." The girl in the picture looked just like Alice. She had shining blue eyes and dark hair. She was beautiful.

Near it was a book I'd been reading. I was so groggy I couldn't even remember the title. But the author's name was staring up at me: Lewis Carroll. The illustration on the front looked bizarre, like something from a hallucination.

"Try to forget about what happened in Alberta," Mom was saying. "There aren't any other monsters around like the Reptile, I guarantee it. He'll never see the light of day again. Remember, you're safe now. Your nightmares are over. British Columbia is a wonderful place."

"It's Lotusland."

"It's Wonderland."

"And," said Mom, "we have a surprise for you." I could see her smiling over at Dad.

"That's right, champ." He smiled back.

"We're going to a resort in a place called Harrison Hot Springs."

"There's only one little catch."

"What's that?" I said, still feeling sleepy.

A phrase was running through my head. *We know, and that's enough.* It was as if someone were whispering it in my ear.

"You have an uncle there: a great-uncle."

"He's kind of weird."

"You should limit your time with him."

"He believes in all sorts of things."

"His name is Walter Middy."

ACKNOWLEDGMENTS

F or his monstrous contribution to this book by way of supplying me with his inimitable knowledge of the Harrison Lake area, and with a stack of wonderful maps, I'd like to thank guide extraordinaire Andreas Sartori of Harrison Hot Springs, Cascade Adventures, and the Bungalow Motel; it is he who truly got Dylan, Alice, and Walter across land to Hell's Gate Canyon. Also to John Green of Harrison Hot Springs, who showed me his sasquatch feet and filled me with wonder about the elusive beast. And to Dr. John A. Bindernagel, the leading scientist in the field of sasquatch research, for his wisdom and encouragement.

More Dylan Maples Adventures

*The Mystery of
Ireland's Eye*

978-1-77108-615-8

*The Secret of
the Silver Mines*

978-1-77108-703-2

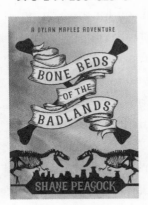

*Bone Beds of the
Badlands*

978-1-77108-658-5

Phantom of Fire

978-1-77108-734-6

ABOUT THE AUTHOR

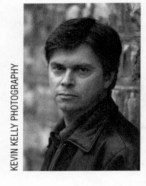

Shane Peacock is a novelist, playwright, journalist, and television screenwriter for audiences of all ages. Among his novels are *Last Message*, a contribution to the groundbreaking Seven Series for young readers, and The Dark Missions of Edgar Brim, a trilogy for teens. His picture book, *The Artist and Me*, was shortlisted for the Marilyn Baillie Award. His bestselling series for young adults, The Boy Sherlock Holmes, has been published in twelve languages and has found its way onto more than sixty shortlists. It won the prestigious Violet Downey Award, two Arthur Ellis Awards for crime fiction, the Ruth & Sylvia Schwartz Award, The Libris Award, and has been a finalist for the Governor General's Award and three times nominated for the TD Canadian Children's Literature Award; as well, each novel in the series was named a Junior Library Guild of America Premier Selection. Visit shanepeacock.ca.